THE WIFE HE CORRECTED

A Clearwater Romance - Book 5

MEGAN MCCOY

Published by Blushing Books
An Imprint of
ABCD Graphics and Design, Inc.
A Virginia Corporation
977 Seminole Trail #233
Charlottesville, VA 22901

Megan McCoy
The Wife He Corrected

Print ISBN: 978-1-63954-102-7
v1

Chapter 1

Joni Sinclair leaned against her sometimes boyfriend as he drove the huge rental truck back home. They'd just been in Zephyrhills, Missouri for a week. The two of them helped move her sister and fiancé into their new apartment and then attended their wedding. She was ready to be home, but couldn't help asking, "Hank, are we really leaving her there?"

"Are you going to cry again?" Hank asked, reaching in his pocket.

"I might," she grabbed the tissue he offered. "It just feels wrong to be so far away from Beth."

"I met all Nick's family. I spent time with them and talked to them. She's going to be safe. Dropped in at the police station with him and we made sure they know what's going on. Nick has friends who work there, too. She's going to be in a bubble of safety." His tone felt so reassuring and for some reason that annoyed her a little.

"I know," Joni tried not to complain. She wasn't complaining. She was rightfully worried about her sister. It was her job.

"But I've done it for three years now. It feels like I'm neglecting my duties or something."

"Joni, you aren't her mother. She has a husband and a new family who will take care of her. You can take care of yourself now."

"I'm fine," she snapped at him. "I already take care of myself!" He could be so sweet, but so insufferable. It was a long way to get back to Clearwater though, so she didn't want to pick a fight with him just yet. It would happen though, she knew, before they got too close. And he just let it. Let her. It had been very sweet of him to take a week out of his life to help her family. How many people would do that? She grabbed her phone from her pocket and texted Beth, *"Are you doing fine?"*

"All good, don't worry. At the airport, getting ready to board the plane for New Orleans. Honeymoon time!"

Joni sighed and put her phone down.

"What's wrong?" Hank asked.

"Nothing," she said, trying her best to keep her tone civil.

"Why don't you try to take a nap?" he said. "It will be about three more hours till we get home."

"Yeah, a nap is what I need," she said, leaning back in her seat and realized he was all she had. Well, not really. He wasn't hers. He seemed happy with their on again, off again relationship. She wasn't. But she wasn't sure what she wanted. Hank was perfect. That was the entire problem.

The man was literally perfect. It was so annoying.

He was gorgeous, tall, dark brown hair, gray-blue eyes that sparkled when he shot her a devastating smile that made butterflies in her stomach and made her want things she'd never wanted before. He taught middle school like she did, he was a Master Gardener, which she wasn't. He baked better bread and cake than professionals could. He cooked and, of course, his grill skills were out of this world. He volunteered to coach Peewee football on top of coaching the junior high team that was part of his job. He was writing a freaking novel. Who does that? As a big brother to his sister, her friend, Ellie, he aced it. He could fix things, he walked his elderly neighbor's dog, and never lost his temper. How could anyone measure up to that? It just wasn't possible, and to top it all off, he was nice. So aggravatingly nice, even when she wasn't.

He did nothing when she threw tantrums, or jumped out of the car, or stormed out of a dinner. Nothing! Just let her be for a few hours or days, then brought her candy, flowers or chocolate and considered it over. And she always let him back in. What was with that? She was tired of living like that, but he seemed to want to do nothing about it. Sometimes she just wanted a little reaction out of him. Why did he just let her walk away from him repeatedly? Did he not care about her enough? Was she just convenient? Handy? Did he sigh, all relieved, when she stormed off and thought, 'don't have to deal with that for a few days' until he wanted, well, what did he want?

Hank Thompson looked over at Joni as she seemed to drift off to sleep. Or fumed. He wasn't sure which. It didn't matter. He needed to get her home before she jumped out the truck and ran away. Keeping her safe was important, even though it was Beth who'd been in danger. He'd keep a close eye on her, though just in case the scum bag lurking around town decided not to take Beth leaving well. They hadn't announced it but word got around. Scumbag Eli's new girlfriend was Miranda and her brother Ben was engaged to Jordyn, who was Joni's good friend. It seemed a far connection but rumors flew in small towns like Clearwater. He needed to keep an eye on Joni and figure out what they were doing. What were they doing?

They'd been on and off again for a couple years now. For a genius, as his sister Ellie told him, sometimes he sure could be dumb. He glanced at her again. She looked like a little angel sleeping, or fuming, there, with her strawberry blonde hair fanned out across the truck seat. Above her adorable little nose, sprinkled with very faint freckles that she always tried to hide, her pretty blue eyes were closed. He had no doubt he was going to marry her one day, once he figured her out. That was the key, though, trying to find out how her little brain ticked. Grinning, he thought, he just might have found the key. They'd find out this next week or so. Find out together. It would work or it wouldn't and either way, he would have at least tried something, because what he was doing now, wasn't working.

He'd gone to Nick's bachelor party while they were in Nick's hometown for the wedding. Nick's brother and friends all taught him a few things about handling women. He'd known these things, but really, while some of these were a part of him, part of how he actually felt, he also knew, you just couldn't do that anymore. Women were equal, more than equal, he knew and you had to treat them as such. That wasn't the issue. The issue was Joni didn't seem happy getting away with the things she did. If she wasn't pleased with the outcome, getting some reward for it, she wouldn't keep doing the same things repeatedly that made her, and him, upset. He knew she didn't like acting like that, throwing fits like a child, but couldn't seem to help herself.

While she wasn't a true redhead like her sister Beth, or Moriah who worked at the bakery on the square, she had a short temper. Really, he doubted hair color had much to do with temper anyway, though he'd never read a study on it, one way or another. Now, when she was teaching, she had a limitless supply of patience. The kids and parents adored her and she excelled at her job. She'd been in town about three or four years now, and had a huge circle of friends, including his sister Ellie. Ellie's group of friends were mostly people she'd known since kindergarten, and now Joni, who fit in as if she had always lived there. He never heard a word about Joni throwing fits with them. In fact, she was the stable one, the calm, mature one.

However, when they were alone, the woman would go off like a firecracker, and sometimes he didn't even know what caused it. But she was soon going to find out what cured it.

Did he dare? Well, they couldn't keep on going the way they were. He was tired of not knowing where he stood, or what she was upset about. He knew she could control her temper everywhere but with him. He had to dare, had to change the dynamic and hopefully for the better.

Today, though, he just needed to get her home. It had been a very stressful week for her, seeing her sister, her best friend, get married and moving and both happening in less than a month. Who got married in a month? But that had been what Beth and Nick wanted, and they made it happen, with a lot of help from Joni. She had to be exhausted, physically and mentally. He felt lucky she hadn't taken his head off, out of sheer stress.

A couple hours later, he reached over and patted her knee. "Almost there, baby, if you want to wake up."

She wiggled in her sleep, and he thought she looked like a sweet little kitten. Then, of course, one who turned into a howling bobcat. Sighing, she sat up, rubbing her eyes and yawning and smiled. "I guess I slept."

"I guess you did," he said. "I'm glad. You needed it."

"I guess," she said. "It has been a long week. Oh, it's raining!"

"Has been for about an hour," he agreed. "And now, look, you have a brand new life ahead of you. You can do anything you want to the house, only worry about you." He tried to sound encouraging.

"I know that," she snapped at him, her kitten side hissing at him. "I know. That doesn't make me worry less about my sister." He could hear her voice rising and decided to change the subject.

"We're almost at the rental place. We'll return the truck, grab the car and you'll be home in less than half an hour. Won't it be nice to sleep in your own bed tonight?"

"Of course it will, we've been gone a week." She folded her arms and stared out the window.

Hank sighed. So she was in that mood. Well, he'd just let her be. Pulling into the rental's parking lot, he pulled the truck next to where his car had been parked, and quickly unloaded their bags from the back, with Joni's help. They both got soaked, the rain coming down in sheets. She yelped once when the thunder cracked, but didn't say anything. They climbed in the car, soaked, and drove up to the office door where he dropped the truck keys in the overnight box.

Getting back in the car, he wiped his face and asked, "Want to hit a drive-thru before we go home?" He could eat. Wet or dry.

She shook her head, without speaking and he half grinned. At least she knew better than to jump out of the car in the rain. "Well, I do. I'm too tired to cook."

Joni looked back from where she'd been staring out the window. "Thank you for coming with me, and being a rock all week. I know I can get grouchy but I really do appreciate you."

Just when he'd thought he'd heard it all. "I'm glad I could be there for you," he said, then placed his order at the speaker.

"It's getting cold," she shivered

"You'd think it was fall," he said. "Almost winter."

Reaching over, he turned the heater up a little for her and added the heated seat for her side. "Better?"

She nodded and he felt bad, wishing he could just tuck her into bed. Instead he handed her the extra sack of fries he'd ordered. "Here you go."

"I said I didn't want anything," she said, but took it from him.

"You're welcome," he said, as mildly as he could. Now was not the time to start the new regime. She'd been pushed to her breaking point.

They headed down the streets of Clearwater and once again he marveled at how much he loved this little town. He couldn't imagine living anywhere else. Growing up here had been picture perfect and one day he hoped his grandkids would come here to visit and maybe settle down. He'd take them to the parks, and to the lake, the local ball games. and wander through the adorable little downtown square. First he needed some kids, before those mythical grandkids showed up, though.

Glancing over to where Joni seemed fascinated by the rain, while methodically eating the fries she didn't want, he opened his mouth to say, well, what? Instead he took a bite of his burger, and realized suddenly how hungry he'd been. After wolfing it down, he pulled into her driveway, which was right next door to his house. They had built a gate in the back yard fence a few years back, to make running back and forth easier. With the rain still sheeting down, you couldn't see either of the gardens, but really, all he cared about was getting her inside and putting her to bed. She probably didn't want him to stay. After a week together, she needed her space. So did he, honestly. He itched to get on his computer and do some research on what the Kinkirk clan, as he thought of them, had talked about.

"Got your keys?" he asked her.

"No, I was just going to walk through the wall," she snapped and he shook his head. Wouldn't be long and they'd be having a discussion about her tone. Feeling half tempted to just grab his bags and head home and let her struggle with her own, he told himself that wasn't what a gentleman did. His mom had raised him right. No matter how tempting it was to let her attitude rub off on him, he just opened his door and grabbed her suitcase from one side while she grabbed two smaller ones from her side and they both rushed across the deck, to the door. He waited while she fumbled with the keys, they walked in and she quickly disarmed the alarm. "Don't forget to turn that back on," he said.

"Yes, Daddy," she said, dropping her bags on the kitchen table. "Thanks, again, Hank. I'm going to take a shower and go to bed."

He bit his tongue not to ask if he could join her. Instead he leaned over and kissed her still wet cheek. "You sleep well, and I'll talk to you tomorrow."

With that he went back out into the rain.

Joni watched him go and yawned, then reset the alarm and made sure her phone had synced up with the camera system. Yup. all was normal. She controlled the urge to call or text Beth again. Beth was fine. Beth was on her honeymoon with her hunky new husband. She did not want her sister bugging her. Who would?

She grabbed her bags and headed up to her bedroom. A hot shower and bed sounded wonderful right now. Halfway wishing that Hank would have insisted on staying tonight, she was also glad he wasn't here. In the mood she was in, she'd be snapping at him again. He didn't deserve that.

Sighing, she stood in the shower letting the hotter than

warm water sluice over her. It did feel good to be home. But what did home really mean anymore? This was their grandmother's house. She and Beth and Sydney for a short time, had moved here over three years ago. She'd left a job she loved, in a city she adored to move to this town. Sure, it was a great little town, and her new job was wonderful. Teaching middle school was always fun and full of surprises. She had a large group of friends. She was getting together with several of them tomorrow for a late lunch which would be fun. Naturally she adored this house where her grandparents had lived. Hobbies, there were a few, her garden, reading, baking, helping Ellie at her events, but yet, there was something missing and she couldn't quite put her finger on it. Now that Beth had left, what was left here in town for her? Her job and the bills that needed to be paid. Well, that settled that, now didn't it? Gotta get those bills paid.

After drying off, she slipped into her robe and headed downstairs and looked in Beth's office. Beth's old office, where she had spent most of her days and many nights until Nick came into her life and whisked her away from here. It looked sparse, empty and forlorn. What would she do with it? She didn't have to decide tonight. Tonight, she was just going to bed.

Hearing her phone beep as she plugged it in, she saw that Hank had sent her a good night text. Sighing, she turned her phone over and turned down her bed covers. She'd spent the week with him, he didn't need to hear from her for a while. It would be best for the both of them, for tonight at least.

"Where's Lucy?" Joni asked Ellie as they walked into Baking Memories together.

"On her way. She went home to let the dogs out for a

minute on her way here," Ellie said, shifting the box in her arms. "She can't wait to hear about Beth's wedding."

"Hi, Jordyn!" Joni said. "Smells good in here."

"Thanks, I like it," Jordyn said. "Welcome home, we missed you!"

"It's good to be home." She watched as Jordyn took her apron off and turned to Moriah. "I'm going to take that break now. If you need me, you know where to find me."

"I'll be fine!" the pretty young redhead told her. "You enjoy your friends."

"Make sure those cupcakes for the Coopers get finished, if you get time."

"Will do," she said. "Have fun!"

"Let's go to the tasting room," Jordyn said. Joni smiled. She liked that cozy little room and noticed, as they walked in, Jordyn had it set up already with four place settings, a pitcher of something, she couldn't tell what, wraps of some kind and a large platter of cookies.

"Oh, Jordyn, this looks great," Joni said, noticing Ellie put her box on the table unpacking four fruit salads. "I feel bad I didn't bring anything now."

"You brought the gossip," Ellie told her. "But don't say anything till Lucy gets here or she'll never forgive us."

They sat down on the comfortable chairs as they heard the bell tinkle at the front door and a cheery call of, "Hello, baby sister, long time no see!"

"Hi, Lucy! Your friends are in the tasting room," they heard Moriah say and a few seconds later, Lucy popped her purple head through the door with a big take out box of pasta salads that she plopped on the table.

"Hey, everybody!" she said. "Hope I'm not late. Gypsy did not want to go outside this afternoon!"

"It is a little chilly and windy and still damp after yesterday's rain. I love your hair!"

"I do, too! Plus Max thinks it's too over the top which makes me like it even better. Nothing more fun than getting a rise out of his stodgy self once in a while!" Lucy said and started dishing salads out into the bowls that Jordyn had set out. "Jordyn, this looks great. I'm starving!"

"Looks like there's plenty," Jordyn said, as Ellie passed the platter of wraps. Soon they were all settled with food and drinks, and Ellie said, "Okay, Joni, we're ready! Let's hear all about the wedding week!"

"Oh, it was so much fun," Joni said. "Well, most of it. We loaded up some of her furniture to move. They're renting an apartment for now, till they find a house, and we got her stuff in. Nick and his brothers had already cleared his cabin out here in town."

"He has brothers? Are they as hot as he is?" Lucy asked.

"Lucy! What would Max think!" Ellie scolded.

"Oh, he knows he's my one and only," Lucy said, "but my eyes still work and you all have to admit that Nick Kinkirk is a hottie."

They all nodded and Joni giggled. "He actually has four brothers, all single," she said. "And a whole slew of cousins, all of them hotter than the rest. There seems to be a preponderance of hot males in that town. In fact, it seemed most of the little kids running around were male too. Must be something in the water!"

Lucy fanned herself. "Oh my. Zephyrhills must be a really fun place to visit!"

"It was," Joni agreed. "It's gorgeous over there. The town is about half the size of Clearwater, and is surrounded by these small rolling hills, and lots of lakes, and well, in the fall, it was breathtaking. It seemed safe and secluded and like its own little island on land."

"So you got her set up in her apartment," Ellie said. "Then?"

"Let's see. Nick's mom, Molly threw her a little bridal shower, and she got to meet all her new friends and neighbors, and some cousins' wives and things. She's going to be surrounded by people who will take care of her."

"That is so good," Ellie said. "I was worried about her going off to a strange town with no one around."

Joni nodded. "It was hard to leave her, but she is going to have lots of protection there. Hank went to Nick's bachelor party and said after meeting everyone he wasn't worried about her anymore. You know how protective Hank is of her."

Lucy sighed. "That's so good. I'm really happy to hear that. So the wedding?"

"The wedding was held in the church where Nick's folks got married and Nick and his brothers were all baptized," Joni started.

"Oh, I think that is so sweet," Jordyn said. "What a family history!"

"It was a gorgeous little church all thick stone and stained glass," Joni said. "Then they had a reception at a local hotel, which was a lot of fun. Hank and I danced all night."

"All those dancing lessons that Mom dragged us to worked for him," Ellie said. "Me, I still have two left feet, but I just follow while Mike leads, so it works."

"When would you have time to go dancing?" Joni teased her. "Anyway, they postponed the honeymoon for a couple days, they want to get settled in. Just headed to New Orleans yesterday, so they are honeymooning as we speak."

"Did your mom go? And Sydney?" Ellie asked.

Joni nodded. "They did, and Mom brought Beth a wedding dress from one of her fancy Chicago stores, off the rack, that fit her like it was made for her. Sydney and I stood up with her, and Mom walked her down the aisle. Nick's brothers stood up with him. It was really nice. One of the cousins owns a flower shop and donated flowers as a wedding present, another made the cake. Which, of course, wasn't as good as yours would have been, Jordyn."

"Of course not," Jordyn agreed. "If she had gotten married here in town I would have made her one."

"I know, but considering the circumstances, we just thought that a small ceremony there would be smarter." Joni picked up a second wrap and took a bite. She hadn't eaten since the fries Hank had given her last night.

"Oh, we agree with that," Ellie said. "But when you and Hank tie the knot, it better be here in town so we can do it up big."

Joni choked on her mouthful of chicken and crunchy vegetables. "Married! No!"

"Are you two fussing again?" Lucy asked. "Doesn't that get tiring? You know you always get back together."

"No, we aren't fussing," Joni said. "I was with him for a week though, and while he was a great help, I'm ready for a little alone time."

"That's what work is for," Lucy told her. "Jordyn, who is going to make your wedding cake?"

"I am," she said. "Who would be better?"

"Set a date yet?" Joni asked.

"We're thinking late winter, early spring, before summer which is a busy season for us both. Between summer weddings and Ben's contracting business, summer will be crazy. I'm not even thinking about taking time off during holiday baking season, which has already started to ramp up."

"Nice thing about being a teacher," Joni said. "Holidays off. Summers are great, laid back, no worries, no work."

"Bad thing about working for the government," Ellie said. "There is no down time, right, Lucy?"

Lucy laughed. "You telling them, Ellie?"

"Telling us what?" Joni asked her.

"Mayor Lydia has decided not to run again, so I am!"

"Are you! Congratulations! This will be so much fun! Sign me up to work on your campaign!" Joni stood up and hugged her. "How excited is Mike?"

Ellie laughed. "What do you think?"

"He supports you in everything you do," Jordyn said. "You know that."

"I do, but he has this weird thing about wanting me home and spending time with him." Ellie rolled her eyes. "Males."

"They're funny, aren't they? Especially your brother," Joni agreed.

"He adores you, you know," Ellie said. "I mean, if taking off for a week and helping someone's sister move isn't love, I don't know what is."

"I know and really, well, it's complicated," Joni said and noticed Ellie looking at her sharply. She was Hank's little sister and while one of her best friends, there were some things you didn't talk to family about.

"Complicated is never good," Lucy shook her purple haired head. "That's one thing I love about Max. I always know right where he stands and right where he wants me standing."

"Max is a good one," Ellie agreed. "And so is Ben. Your mountain man is a sweetheart, Jordyn, even if Miranda is his sister."

"That's not his fault!" Jordyn said. "Besides, I rarely have to see her and I actually refuse to go anywhere with that new boyfriend of hers. Ben understands that."

Joni gave a huge shudder at that. Miranda's boyfriend was the reason her sister had left town. No one but Miranda could stand Eli. "Ugh. I just thought, she will be at your wedding, won't she?"

"Since she's about all the family he has, I imagine so. Maybe she will break up with the scum bag before then."

"We can only hope," Lucy said, picking up her glass. "Here's to Jordyn's fun wedding with no drama!"

"Cheers!" They clinked glasses and took a sip.

"So do you have any big plans now that you're rattling around that big house all by yourself?" Jordyn asked.

Joni shook her head. "It still doesn't seem real, you know. Like I'll pop my head in her office and she'll be in there pounding away on her computer."

"Well, it's only been, what, one day since you got back? You'll get used to it. Unless you and Hank decide to move in together or something."

Laughing at that thought, Joni said, "We'd kill each other. Having our own space makes us both happier, I think."

Lucy shook her head. "That would make me tired. I don't like volatile."

"I don't either," Joni said. "He's just so frustrating!"

"Yeah, frustrating isn't a good way to live," Ellie agreed. "I know Mike gets frustrated with me sometimes, though he's pretty patient until he's not. When he's done, I know about it!"

"See, Hank doesn't seem to do that. I can do anything I want and he just lets me. It's like he doesn't care enough. I don't know what I'd want him to do, in any case, but just something, you know?"

Lucy reached over and patted her hand. "I do know. Hope you guys can figure something out, or maybe he just isn't the one for you."

"Ugh, don't say that, Lucy! I want Joni to be my sister!"

"We're already sisters," Joni told her. "Me marrying your brother or not won't change that."

"Well, it would be more legal or something," Ellie said, reaching for a cookie. "Lucy and I have to get back to work, but let's get all the guys and do something at my house next week, okay?"

They all nodded, helped Jordyn clean up and soon Joni

was on her way out, heading to the grocery store. She needed to refill some staples before she had to be back at work tomorrow. Hank had already gone back today, they had both used sick and personal days to take off for the move and the wedding and she'd taken an extra day to decompress, or if she'd needed, to stay a little longer with Beth. Beth who did not seem to need her anymore and it was disconcerting to say the very least. This was now her life and she had a good one. She could actually do anything she wanted after the school year ended, but she had no desire to leave Clearwater. Or did she?

Where would she go? To Zephyrhills with Beth and Nick? That would just be odd. Her mom was too settled and fulfilled with work in northern Chicago to be any good company for her, and had her own social life. Well, she assumed she did. Sydney was in her last year of veterinary school and just crazy busy. Besides, who knew where she'd end up after she graduated. Apparently she'd been offered several jobs already. No reason to move close to her.

No, this is where she'd stay, unless like Beth, she met someone and ran off. Half smiling, she thought of Hank. Again. She couldn't really imagine life without Hank in it. She just needed something more than he could give her. Right now, though, she'd give him supper after his first day back. Picking up some pork chops, she threw them in her cart. It was chilly out, but Hank had been known to grill out in the snow. Chilly wouldn't stop him. She'd get home and start marinating.

Since Beth had announced she and Nick were getting married and moving, in a month, all she'd done was ruminate and she was getting a little tired of it. How much deep introspection did one woman need? She'd had plenty of it. Maybe they'd just have a fun evening, play some cards, not fight. What were the odds of that?

Slim and none, of course, she found out a few hours later.

"We need to talk," Hank told her as they cleared the dinner dishes.

"Isn't that the female's line?" she said, filling the sink with soap and hot water.

"My female doesn't like to talk," he said, picking up a dish towel.

"Huh. That's odd. I wonder why that is? Most females do. Maybe you are hard to talk to?"

He shook his head. "No, I'm sure that's not it. I give her a lot of space and a lot of room and chances. I try to be a safe place for her, but it doesn't seem to be making her happy."

Joni felt her heart beat faster. Was he breaking up with her? It would serve her right. "It doesn't sound like it's you, then," she agreed. "What do you think is wrong with her?"

"Well, I've learned a lot this past week while we've been gone. Listened to a lot of guy talk."

Joni rolled her eyes. "I'm sure the sex isn't the problem I've heard rumors you actually overachieve in that department."

Hank laughed and popped her bottom with the towel, making her squeal and sort of smile despite the sting. Maybe he wasn't breaking up with her? What was he doing then?

"No, it wasn't about sex. As you've heard the rumors, then you might already know that that isn't the problem."

"Then whatever could it be?" she asked him draining the sink and wiping it dry.

"I don't give her a wall to lean against," he said.

Joni shook her head. "Well, if I don't understand what that means, I'm sure your hypothetical female won't either."

"She's not hypothetical, and that's the problem. I'm sort of in love with her and I'm pretty sure she feels the same about me, but she keeps picking these silly little fights and acting like a child. Any ideas why she'd do that?"

"Because she can?" Joni swallowed hard. Where was he going with this?

"Exactly." He took her by the arm and moved her to a kitchen chair, and sat her down. "And that ends today."

He pulled out his chair and sat close to her. "What does that even mean?" she asked, noting her fingers were trembling.

"I'm planning to give her a wall to lean against, shove against and know it will be unmoving and sturdy for her. For you."

"I'm still very confused. What is this wall for and why am I shoving?" She liked it better when there was the safety net of some other person in this conversation. However weird it sounded.

"You are shoving because the wall keeps moving. You jump out of the car and the wall drives away. You walk out of dinner and the wall pays the bill, let's you cool off and appeases you. The wall is done with all that. You know how to behave. You are an excellent teacher. You have a large social network. I watched you all week and the only person you snapped at even once was me. It was a very stressful situation and yet, you handled everything, even your mother, with good grace and humor. Then turned around and snapped all over me."

Yeah. She knew that. Why did she do that? Perfect Hank probably knew.

"Well, since you know everything, explain this to me. Why?"

"Because I let you and because you don't feel safe with me."

Joni shook her head. "Henry, that makes no sense at all.

Maybe you are the only one I do feel safe with, so I can act out."

"Are you happy when you have your little tantrums?" he asked.

"I'm unhappy with you and that's why I'm doing it," she said. "You can be so frustrating and just make me crazy."

"So we agree, it's my behavior that makes you act like you do."

"Yes!" she said, almost triumphantly. "It is!"

"That's why I'm changing my behavior." He crossed his arms and looked at her steadily.

Joni sighed in exasperation. "What does that even mean?" Why was he being so cryptic? The man was a teacher and a literal genius. Surely he could find words to use.

"What part confused you?" He looked at her steadily and once again she marveled at how handsome and hot he was. She could get lost in those eyes. And kissing those lips and, well... Whatever else he decided to do.

"What behavior are you changing?" See, she knew how to use words.

"The behavior that allows you to get away with things and then feel bad about it," he said.

"Let me? Umm, well, as far as I know, I'm a grown adult who doesn't need permission to act anyway I choose to act." She shoved a wisp of hair back away from her eyes where it had strayed.

"You are right, I agree. But what happens if you break the law?"

"Well, if you get caught, you get a ticket, or a fine, or even go to jail. You planning to give me a ticket if I don't behave to your standards?" She could feel her tone becoming mocking. She didn't like when she did that. It made her uncomfortable but for some reason he just brought it out of her. No one else did for some reason, just him. Why, now, was the million dollar question.

"No, but you are going to have consequences, if you still think we should be together."

"Well, of course we should be together," she snapped again, and tried to soften her tone. "I mean, we enjoy each other, our lifestyles fit, you know, all the usual stuff that we've talked about before."

"I'm going to take steps to make our life together better," he said. "You know we have talked occasionally about a little more, about being actually together and," he held his hand up as she started to protest, silencing her, "and we both know we aren't ready for that yet, right?"

She nodded, heart hammering so fast she hoped it would calm down before it burst as he continued, "So I've found a couple ways to deal with it."

"Deal with what? Your behavior?" She felt even more confused than she had before.

"No, your behavior. Well, both. I'm changing the way I behave to change the way you behave. We both know we aren't happy like this, so change is starting now."

"You are irking me with your cryptic comments," she said and looked over at the stove, wondering when the last time she cleaned the oven was. Probably needed it again. She jerked as he put a large hand on the top of her head, tightened his fingers and moved it so she could look at him. Umm, what was with this?

"You are going to be more than irked in a few minutes," he said, and let go of her head. "Now. We are both in agreement we want this relationship, right?"

Where had her laid back, take anything man gone? This was not him and she didn't know why, but it gave her a shiver of excitement. Why not, she should see where this went. What's the worst that could happen?

"Sure. I mean, I don't want to break up if that's what you're asking."

"And you agree what we are doing isn't working as well as it should and that we aren't as happy as we could be?"

That one was a given. "Yes, I do agree with that."

"Do you think actions should have consequences?"

"Well, mostly, but sometimes…" her voice trailed off. Where was this going?

"Sometimes, what?" he asked.

Joni shrugged, feeling remarkably like a naughty kid at the principal's office. It made her feel strange, nervous, yet a little excited and somehow turned on.

"Do you think you should get away with the way you treat me and how you act sometimes when we're together?" He still had his hand on her head so she couldn't move and was looking directly into his deep eyes.

She tried to shake her head but his hand wouldn't let her move it. "Not really," she admitted. "But, well, sometimes you just frustrate me so much."

"You don't think it's frustrating to me when you throw tantrums like a child?"

"I do not throw tantrums," she protested, wishing he'd let go of her head.

"What do you call it then?"

"Walking away from the situation before I do or say something I'll regret," she admitted. Where was he going with this?

"From now on, your actions are going to have consequences."

"Like what?" she asked, suddenly fascinated.

"Anytime you throw yourself a little fit–" He finally let go of her head and reached into his jeans pocket and pulled out a quarter. "You know what to do with this?"

This time she shook her now freed head. "Vending machine for coffee?"

"Nope. It's for your nose."

"Umm, what?" Now she felt thoroughly confused.

"You take your quarter and go to the closest wall and hold your little nose on it till you calm down. Then you're going over my knee and I'll be turning your adorable butt as red as your sister's hair."

Joni let out a peal of giggles, and when she could catch her breath, said, "You have got to be kidding. Right?" She looked into his eyes and suddenly it didn't seem funny anymore. "Right?"

Chapter 2

"**D**o I look like I'm kidding?"

"Well, no, but you have to be, right? I mean, that just isn't a thing!"

"You'd be surprised how often it is a thing," he said, and put the quarter in the middle of the table. Her eyes stared at it, fascinated.

"What if I don't want to basically stand in the corner?"

"That's the point. You don't want to, especially when you realize what's going to come after."

"After?" What was wrong with her brain? This conversation was not processing well.

"As soon as you drop the quarter, or I tell you it's time, you'll go over my knee."

This time her head shake felt almost violent in denial. "Am not! Hank, that is the most asinine thing I've ever heard!"

"Is it? My theory is that it will calm you down and settle your nerves and if I do it properly, and, little lady, I will do it very properly, you'll think twice before you have another fit." He leaned back and crossed his arms. "Any questions?"

"Oh, about a million," she said as sarcastically as she could muster. "Like no and hell no."

"And yet," he said.

"Yet what? Henry David Thompson, this is not an option!"

"It's a very viable option. I imagine you are going to be surprised at the results."

Joni kept shaking her head till she thought her brains would rattle. "I don't think so because this isn't going to happen."

"So we continue on like we have been? Having us both miserable?"

"We aren't miserable all the time!" she said.

"Why should we be miserable at all?"

What could she say to that? "Sounds like I might be miserable standing in the corner and then, well, you know—" She couldn't bring herself to say it.

"Then getting your bottom paddled?" he filled in. "It's not to make you miserable, it's to help reset your brain, so you don't make us unhappy anymore. Because you know, one of these days when you stomp away, one of us won't be coming around again. I think we mean too much to each other for that to happen."

She shook her head almost automatically which she noticed made him almost smile. "You don't think we do?"

"Of course we do. It just won't happen!"

"We are both in agreement on that," he said. "So I'm making sure it doesn't happen. Does that make sense in your stubborn little head?"

Joni didn't want to admit it. "It just isn't a thing!" she protested again.

"It is now," he said, and picked up the quarter to put it back in his pocket. "You just think on this tonight. It will come to you. I sent some links to your phone, if you want to research."

"You are so thoughtful," she mumbled, wishing he'd leave so she could look at her phone.

"Oh, you have no idea," he said, and stood up. "I'm going home. You have tonight to think about it. I have to be at work early for practice in the morning, but we can have dinner tomorrow night. You come over, I'll cook."

She nodded, not certain if she trusted her voice or not. He walked over and pulled her arm so she stood up, then tugged her into her arms. "Relax, baby, this is a good thing for us both."

Yeah, that was easy for him to say! He wasn't going to be the one standing in the corner or getting their bottom blistered. She shook her head slightly and he laughed. "You'll see. See you tomorrow night." And with that, he smacked her butt and walked out the back door while she watched. "Don't forget to set the alarm."

Why would she forget to set the alarm? Did he think she went crazy all of a sudden or something? Just because Beth wasn't here, didn't mean things were suddenly safe. She knew that. She set the alarm and put a cup of water in the microwave to heat for tea, and rummaged for the box of popcorn she knew was in the cabinet somewhere. A few minutes later, she carried her sustenance into the cozy living room and settled in the large rocker recliner. Only then did she turn her phone on and start scrolling the links.

Two hours later, her tea cold and the popcorn untouched, she put the phone down on the table and walked to the window to stare out at the street. What was he thinking? Had he gone insane all of a sudden? She never even read the fifty shades books! And here he was wanting her to live it. He was a middle school teacher, not a billionaire with a shady past! She didn't have a kinky bone in her body, that she knew of, anyway.

Yet, there was something in her that niggled at her brain, wondering, wanting. No, not wanting. Wanting to reject it. However, she sighed and turned away from the window and the rain pouring down. It had been so pretty earlier but that was Illinois weather for you. You just never knew what it was going to do when. There was school tomorrow. She should get ready for bed. Her mind raced though and she wasn't certain she could settle down enough to go to sleep. Flipping the TV on, she sat back down in the recliner and stared at the people hunting for beachfront houses with their kajillion dollar budgets. The ocean would be lovely. Standing against the wall, holding a quarter on it with her nose, would not be. It would be humiliating and ridiculous, and then knowing that after, she was to willingly go over his knees? And then, he would… well, that made no sense at all.

Was she willing to break up with him over it? Was this a deal breaker for both of them? Would he break up with her if she didn't agree to this? Well, it was her own fault. She knew how to behave. Why didn't she? Was she wanting a reaction? Probably, but not like this! What if she walked out on him during a meal, as she'd done half a dozen times before? Would he drag her back in the restaurant and stand her against the wall? Wait till they got home? What if he did nothing?

Yeah, what if he did nothing after saying he would? How would that make her feel? Relieved she got away with it or upset that he didn't follow through? Why would she be upset? Grown people didn't get punished! Well, like that anyway. Though, she'd been reading and well, it seems many did, and not only did, but consented to it and appreciated it. Or something. This whole entire thing seemed too weird. She knew, realized, she'd have to consent to all this if it were to happen and if it were to work. He couldn't physically force her to stand in the corner. He could, however, force a spanking on her. Would he? Suddenly, she just didn't know.

What was she going to do?

Looking down at her phone, she noted the time. Almost midnight and she had to work in the morning. She really needed to go to bed, despite knowing that sleep would be very elusive tonight.

Sighing, she wondered if she just bit down her frustration with him and didn't act out, if this would all just go away. That seemed the best idea. It was probably his evil plan anyway! Okay, that's what she would do then. Going into her room, she spied a handful of change on her dresser, and grabbed a quarter. Staring at it, she walked over to the wall and placed it against the wall, then pushed her nose against it. She stared at the dusty rose paint on the wall. It was a pretty color. It should be, she picked it out. Beth's room was a light blue, Sydney's was still covered in the old wallpaper their grandmother had put on. Syd hadn't been here long enough to change anything. This was boring. How long would he make her stand here? Till she mentally inventoried the attic, too?

What would he do when she was done holding the quarter to the wall? Would he really put her across his lap and spank her? Would it hurt? She couldn't imagine Hank hurting her. Would it be bad? Would she cry? That seemed improbable too. Yeah, she put her finger on the quarter and stepped back, dropping it back on the pile.

Okay, she made a decision. She'd agree to this and then just not do anything that deserved what he would consider to be a corner standing, spanking offense. He was the only one she behaved like that toward anyway. It couldn't be that hard, could it?

She wished she could talk to someone about it, but really, who? Her best friends included Ellie who was Hank's sister.

No way could she tell Ellie her brother was a kinkster! If that was what he even was. Lucy, while delightful and funny and sweet as the day was long, would never understand! It would never cross sweet little Lucy's mind that someone would want to spank her. Jordyn? No. Newly engaged, planning a wedding, finishing up her apartment over the bakery and running her own business, well, she had enough on her plate. Besides, it might scare her off marriage if she thought grown women got spanked! How did she not know of any of this? Apparently it was a big, huge, underground, secret thing she, and her friends, had no idea existed. Maybe Clearwater was this little safe haven of non-spanking males. Well, until now.

What would people at school think if they knew what he wanted to do to her? Well, actually, not much more than they thought now, probably. They seemed to be a source of amusement to their friends. "Do you and Hank want to come over, you know, if you are still together that day." Or "So, are you on again or off again this week?" She didn't think they broke up that much, but apparently other people saw it differently. He could just be so annoying!

Her mind raced, but she kept coming back to, 'just agree and behave'. Of course, she could do that, she'd have to do that. Because if she agreed, she'd have to follow through and suffer the consequences if she didn't behave, otherwise what good would her word be? It wouldn't. Sure, it would be a little stressful on her, but not nearly as stressful as standing in the corner, knowing what was coming after she got out of the corner.

Finally, she fell into a fitful sleep, and waited for the alarm to go off way too early.

Getting home from school the next day, she placed her laptop on the kitchen table and flipped it open. There would be no supper cooking tonight, Hank said he was cooking and they both knew he was the much better cook of the two of them. That was part of the reason he was so annoying. There wasn't anything he couldn't do and do well. Yes, and mostly better than she could. Who wouldn't get frustrated with that? And he was like Spock. All logic, all the time. It was weird this idea of his was so, well, physical. So out of character for him. What was with this?

Joni flipped through a few more links she'd bookmarked from last night's research, then stood up to go change and get ready for the evening. She had no homework to grade tonight and it felt like a night off. The weather outside was crisp and cool. Perfect fall weather. Illinois winters weren't much fun, but fall was often invigorating and there was always spring to look forward to.

Going upstairs, she stopped in the hallway and looked at Beth's bedroom door. She'd swear it was closed this morning when she went to work. She always kept Sydney's bedroom's door shut on the theory that it wouldn't get dirty that way, and when the heater came on she could shut off the vents. Not heating a room in this big house was helpful for the large power bill, and now that Beth moved out, she'd done the same thing to her room. She glanced over. Syd's door was still closed.

Joni felt a little thrill of nerves as she walked into the room, turned the light on, and looked around. She looked under the bed and heart hammering, into the almost empty closet. No, nothing looked moved and nothing looked out of place. Had she turned the alarm on this morning? She always turned the alarm on. Flipping the light off, she pulled the door closed with a hard click. Okay. It was probably just the house settling. Nothing more. It was an old house, after all, and old houses did things like settle and creak. She'd gotten so she enjoyed the creaking of the old settling house. Probably a door swinging open was one of those things. She'd review the camera tapes, just in case, but felt fairly sure this was a non-issue. It better be. The alternative was too frightening to even think about.

Just in case, though, she checked out her room and then changed clothes into jeans and a warm sweater for dinner with Hank. Already she seemed to be focused on him and not the door that surely meant nothing. She hoped things, the conversation, would go smoothly tonight. Why wouldn't it? He was getting what he wanted. She planned to agree to this idea of his and then never give him cause to implement it. What could go wrong, and more importantly, what was he making for supper? She was starving!

Heading to the kitchen door, she double checked it behind her, making sure the alarm was on and set. It was. She always did that, the bedroom door was a fluke, nothing more, and she put it out of her mind as she headed to what was going to be an enjoyable night and a peaceful dinner.

She shivered a little, noticing it was already starting to get dark, but there were too many clouds to see much of a sunset. Taking a deep breath, she walked across the deck. Sometimes she missed the big back porch that used to be there, but not the critters that liked to live under it, or the rotting wood smell when they came out. The deck was lovely and very handy. It held a small table and four chairs, a BBQ grill and even a corn hole game that she enjoyed. It was one thing she was almost as good at as Hank was. She almost skipped through the back yard and over to the gate they'd installed when they did the deck. She and Hank were back and forth so much, it had just seemed more practical than going around the fence and through the front doors of each other's houses. They were both more back door people, coming into kitchens and pouring a glass of sweet tea and settling down at the table for a chat and a cookie. She hoped he made some bread for tonight. He showed her his recipe and even walked her through the steps several times, but hers still never came out as well as his. He just had a touch for it. He had a touch for a lot of things, except handling her properly, she guessed as she knocked on the back door to his house, then walked in.

As always it smelled so good in his house. He was always baking something or drying herbs he grew or displaying the flowers from his garden. His kitchen felt even more comfortable and homey than hers did, and she loved her kitchen. His was a little more sleek and modern than hers, thanks to all his constant renovation of the house. The cabinets were all white, the floors a wonderful honey oak, the appliances were stainless steel and never seemed to have fingerprints on them. There was a wine fridge built in and a big pantry that always seemed over full to her, considering he was just one person.

"Hank," she called out. "I'm here."

"Be right down," he called back. She poked around in the kitchen, looking in the pans on the stove and peeking in the oven. Chicken Cordon Bleu and rice pilaf, roasted asparagus. Was there anything he didn't do to perfection? He could be so irritating. However, she wasn't letting him irritate her. That was a her problem, not a him problem. She was an adult and would act like it. No matter how irritatingly perfect he was.

He walked in, obviously freshly showered in his jeans, t-shirt and bare feet, hair still wet. "Hey, Joni. Glad to see you," he said.

"Hey, handsome," she said, smiling at him. See, not irritated at all! "Looking really good."

"Little ol' me?" he said, walking over to the stove. "You're too kind."

"Aren't I though? What can I do to help?"

"Get the wine from the fridge and pour us both a glass, if you want," he said. "This will be done in a few minutes."

"Sure," she said and went to the built in wine fridge, and pulled out a bottle of wine with a name she recognized. Of course, no boxes of wine for him! Luckily, she had opened a few bottles during her lifetime. She opened the drawer, where, of course, everything was in order. Grabbing the opener, she popped the cork, and poured it into the two wine glasses, adding a little more to hers. She and her lovely new attitude deserved it!

Taking a sip, she put the glasses down on the table and grabbed the plates from the cabinet. They worked in easy rhythm in silence, as she listened to the soothing sounds of the classical jazz he often had playing in the house. From where? She didn't know for sure, but since he was always messing with something in the house, he probably had a secret sound system rigged in the walls. After last night's tossing and turning and worrying and anxiety, she suddenly felt soothed and much calmer. He had that way about him, for not only her, some-times, when he wasn't irritating the heck out of her, but the kids he taught and the neighbors he helped.

"You are a good man, Henry Thompson," she told him as he picked up the plates she'd put down and carried them to the stove.

"Because I can cook? Low standards there, Joni," he said as he put the rice down then the chicken on top of it and the roasted asparagus beside it.

"Yes, because I am that shallow. It's the only thing I really care about, getting my stomach well filled."

"Glad I can fill that role for you," he said, putting the plates down and sitting down beside her.

"Glad you can, too," she said. "How was school today?"

"Really good, you?"

"I swear I'm going to have to send Ayden White to the office or call his mother or you need to give him more laps at practice. He has more pent up energy than six kids need."

Hank nodded. "Yeah, his folks are going through a divorce and he's had a lot piled on him at home taking care of his little sisters while the fall out is going on. He's overreacting at school because that's the only safe place he can do it. But you might be right, he might need a little more energy output to help handle his stress. I'll look into that."

Joni felt a pang. She should have thought of that, something at home, and usually she would, but the kid had gotten on her last nerve so many times lately, it was hard to see past the behavior this time. "I'll keep that in mind," she said. "How did you find out?"

"I see his dad at the ball games," he said. "He came over and told me."

That made sense. "I'll try to contact his mom and see if she needs any help or anything, then," Joni said. "Thank you for telling me that. Gives me a new perspective."

"Speaking of perspective," he said, cutting up his asparagus. "What did you decide about my little proposition?"

Joni took a deep breath, which weirdly seemed shaky to her. Why? There was nothing to be worried about after all. "Since the goal for both of us is to have a calmer and more smooth relationship, to be happy together, and since you seem to think you have a solution, I agree for a trial period."

"A trial period?"

"Yes. In three months if we are still unhappy, if nothing has changed, we revisit this conversation and either try something different, or well, you know."

He nodded. "And if it is working?"

"Hank, I really don't want the threat of a spanking hanging over my head all my life!"

He laughed. "You do have a cute little butt. I bet it's going to look adorable all wiggly over my lap while you learn the error of your ways."

"Is that the goal? For you to see my butt?"

"Not the goal, but a perk," he said.

Joni tried not to smile. "Have you done this before?" she asked.

"Spanked?" She nodded and held her breath. Why? She didn't know.

He shrugged. "Never in this context but I have a little paddle that has been used a few times, but just for playtime."

"Playtime?" she gasped. "What's fun about a spanking?"

"Remind me to show you later how much fun they can be," he said. "But for the purpose we're talking about it won't be fun. It will be for correction."

Her fork stopped halfway to her mouth. "Did I agree to that?"

"You did," he said, looking her right in the eye and making her squirm. Yeah, she had.

"But only if I have what you call a tantrum, right? Not just because you want to? So if I'm good, and don't let your perfection make me insanely frustrated, then I won't get one."

"Oh, so it's my fault?" He raised his eyebrows at her and she smiled again.

"Well, you didn't think it was mine, did you?"

"I realized I had a hand in it but didn't realize it was because I was so perfect," he said.

"Well, now you know," she said. "Well?"

"I promised you a fun playtime spanking sometime in the future, but yes. As long as you behave and don't throw a tantrum like jumping out of the car and Ubering home, or stomping out of a restaurant, then your little nose and bottom will be safe."

She'd forgotten about the standing against the wall thing. Yeah. "I don't understand the concept behind that. I mean, I get the spanking thing, but why the nose thing?"

"Well, the reason you throw these little fits is because you get yourself all worked up, and can't calm yourself down for some reason. The corner time is to settle you down, give you some time to think and a little time to worry about how your actions will be affecting your bottom very soon."

"Worry?" she asked, feeling very weak and vulnerable all of a sudden.

"I am pretty sure if you are standing against the wall with your nose holding up a quarter and your pants down by your ankles you'll worry some."

"You didn't say anything about that!" she said, shaking her head, trying to visualize that sight. Nope!

"Sure I did. When I see you starting to get worked up, I'll reach in my pocket and hand you a quarter. Now, if we're out, then you just hold onto it until we get home, then march yourself to the nearest wall, or the wall I tell you to, and then drop your pants and hold the quarter until I'm ready to paddle you properly."

"But, my pants!"

He shrugged. "You won't be needing them. Good spankings are given on a bare bottom so I can have proper aim and make sure you get some very nice color."

Joni buried her face in her hands. "This does not sound like a good time at all," she complained.

"Yet, you agreed to it and you know how you can avoid it."

She sighed. "I guess."

"What are you guessing?" He reached over and pulled her hands away from her face, then kissed them both as he held them. "This will be a good progression toward our future happiness."

"That's because you won't be having the paddle applied to your bare backside," she said.

"See how fast you've come to accept it," he said. "Chocolate cheesecake?"

Of course he'd made chocolate cheesecake. Why not?

She got up to clear the plates while he opened the refrigerator and pulled out and sliced the cheesecake. They worked pretty well together. Why couldn't it be like this all the time?

"Want to take it to the couch in the living room?" he asked. "Start a fire?"

Could there be anything more perfect than snuggling on the couch, watching the fire and eating cheesecake? She didn't think so. "More wine? Some decaf coffee? You don't need caffeine this late at night," he asked. Or said. She wasn't clear on why he thought that, but he was right, she didn't.

"Coffee sounds good. I'll take the plates into the living room."

"Good girl," he said. "I'll be right there with the coffee."

Good girl? What was with that? She just shook her head and carried the plates to the long table in front of the couch and pulled out the coasters for the coffee mugs soon to come, then knelt in front of the fire to start it. He'd shown her how he liked it done, aka The Only Proper Way. How had she not realized how bossy he was? Well, not really bossy, just thought he knew everything. The sad thing was, he really did seem to know almost everything and what he didn't know today, he'd know by tomorrow if it came up in a conversation or something. He had wicked research skills and his memory was phenomenal.

"What did you Google to come up with all this?" she asked, sitting back on her heels to watch the fire catch.

"All what?" He put the coffee cups down on the coasters, then came over and helped her up and leaned down to do something to the fire. Make sure it was perfect, she assumed, or correct something she did.

Settling on the couch, she said, "All this corner time spanking stuff. Did you Google how to make your girlfriend behave or something?"

"Basically," he said. "I heard a conversation from one of

Nick's married cousins while we were at the wedding and he was telling his cousins how his wife earned herself a bruised butt just a few days before."

"Bruises? He leaves bruises on his wife?"

"When you hit something with a paddle hard enough a few times, bruises happen." Hank finished fixing whatever fire mistake she'd made and came over to sit down beside her. "Couple of the others were talking about how short or long a time it had been since their wives or girlfriends had needed a good blistering."

"Blistering?" she interrupted shaking her head with the cheesecake bite halfway to her mouth. "I'm liking this less and less all the time." She put the cheesecake in her mouth and it almost melted. Once again, perfection.

"Entirely consensual," he assured her. "Although I'm sure there are a few minutes when it doesn't feel like it."

"Oh, I'm sure there are," she murmured and put another bite in her mouth.

"Well, if you are doing it right," he said. "But anyway, one of the women, and I wasn't clear who, there were so many of them, actually brings the hairbrush to her guy every morning."

Joni felt confused. "Hairbrush?"

"That's his favorite implement," Hank said, then sipped his coffee. "He said their relationship did a complete 180 since she started getting a daily paddling. Keeps her behavior in line and lets her know who's in charge."

"Are you wanting to be in charge?" Joni's mind raced. This was a lot more than stopping a couple little tantrums, she was figuring out.

"We will see about that, but then I came home and ran across DD, which means domestic discipline. Some of those were the links I sent you."

She nodded. "I guess. So this happens a lot?"

"More than you'd realize," he said. "It's new to me. I've paddled before, but just in fun or as foreplay, but not to change or correct a behavior. We will see how it works, though."

"So I'm the guinea pig?"

Hank set his coffee down and laughed. "Yeah, I guess so. Congratulations."

"Thanks?" she said. "You know my plan is to not act up and never have that happen, don't you?"

He put his arm around her and she snuggled close to him. "I do realize that, however I know you and it won't be a week before you test me."

"Test you? What does that even mean?"

"You're a teacher, you know what a test is. But you'll act out, just to see if I'll follow through."

"Will not."

"Will, too. Want to bet on it?"

"Yes. What do you want to bet?"

"Floor cleaning," he said promptly. "You know mopping floors are not my favorite thing to do. If I win and you end up in the corner for a real reason and not a made up one, I'll mop and buff all your floors. If I win and you throw a tantrum, then you will do the same to mine."

"It's a deal." Joni reached over to shake his hand to seal it. "My floors need a good buffing."

"I know they do," he said. "Too bad I won't be doing it for you."

Joni rolled her eyes. Mr. Perfection Know It All had spoken.

Joni got ready to head out to dinner at Ellie's. She'd had a long day at work, even staying late to talk to Ayden's mother and that hadn't gone well. She'd cried, talking about being a stay at home mom for over ten years and how hard it was to find a decent job with decent hours at her age with nothing on her resume. Despite what people tried to spout, employers were not impressed with her domestic engineering experience. Right now she was working retail which was strange and odd hours, different all the time, and Ayden had to step up and watch his two little sisters more often than she was comfortable with. But, like she said, the kids had to eat and have a roof over their heads. While their dad was giving her child support, it wasn't enough to keep them in the home they'd always been in, and they'd had to move out of the house into a small apartment. Joni shook her head, feeling bad for the desperation she saw on the woman's face. She felt very glad she had a skill she could always fall back on. Would she want to be a stay at home mom? She didn't really think so, for very long at least. Relying totally on someone else for her income and socialization would be challenging for her and keeping her temper around Hank was challenging enough right now.

He was picking her up to take her to Ellie's for dinner and she grabbed the fruit salad she'd made before school to take with her. He'd probably bring bread or rolls. Where he found time to bake with everything else he did, she never could figure out. However, he seemed to find or make the time and his house always smelled fantastic, like lovely yeasty rolls and rising bread, and well, just the smell of him. He had his own scent and she simply adored it. When they were close, she always tried to sniff the good smells out of him. Sometimes she thought she got most of it, but he regenerated more. Because, of course, he was perfect and that is what perfect people did.

She smiled. Tonight would be a fun night, with friends, and nothing more. No stress, no worries and she certainly wasn't going to let Hank push her buttons. If this party went like most of them, they'd separate as soon as they arrived, he'd go to the patio if it wasn't raining and it looked like it might, or the garage where Mike had a nice little bar area set up. She'd, of course, hang out in the kitchen with the women until supper when they all came back together to eat and then would spend the evening together, chattering over desserts and drinks, hopefully in front of Mike and Ellie's huge fireplace. She did love a fire, especially with Hank's arm around her. One thing about him, she rolled her eyes at her own thoughts, well, of course he was the best snuggler ever. What didn't he do right and perfectly? "Don't even go there, Joni Suzanne," she scolded herself out loud. "No one is perfect and the last thing you need is to be getting pre-irritated at him!"

They were three days into their weeklong bet. She was almost halfway through it and her floors would appreciate the Henry perfection as he buffed. She'd sit down with a glass of wine and cheer him on. It was her plan. She sure didn't want to mop and buff his floors. One, his house was bigger than hers and two, he was much pickier than she was. All she had to do was not test him.

Of course, as much as she most emphatically did not want any of that from the floors to the corner to the spanking that sounded less and less interesting to her all the time, she was curious about it. The entire thing. Well, not the floors. Would he really make her stand in the corner holding a quarter with her nose and her pants around her ankles? Would she really put her over his knee and paddle her? How would it work? Would she even fit over his lap? Awkward was the only way she imagined it feeling. Don't forget painful, she reminded herself. If she knew Hank as well as she thought she did, he would spank like he did everything else, thoroughly and well and properly. Make sure the job was completely finished before he stopped. After it was over, she'd know what a real spanking felt like and for some reason it intrigued her, just a little, not that she'd ever ever admit that to anyone. Especially not Hank who would laugh and offer to help her find out. What would that fun spanking be like? She'd never done that, even during foreplay.

Taking off her work clothes, she pulled on jeans and a soft fleece hoodie which would be comfortable and nice if it rained and slipped on her sneakers. Perfectly comfortable for a night hanging out with friends. The hoodie was long enough to look more tunic like and she refused to consider she might be doing it for a reason. If her pants were around her ankles, it would cover parts. Not that it was in the remote realm of possibilities, of course. She just liked it and liked the color and nothing more.

She had no desire to 'test' him and see if he would follow through on his promise, or threat. The desire to buff his floors was even less. So, tonight she'd be all strawberries and cream, smiles and giggles. Even tempered and just going along with the flow. If she wanted to test him, which she didn't, she could do that in four days. There was no reason to do it tonight. Hopefully he could keep his irritating perfection down to a low simmer. Some days he ramped it up, just because, she felt certain. Or just to irk her. Or... well, she just didn't know why he did it, but she knew he did it on purpose.

Walking back to the kitchen, she covered the fruit salad and put it in a small cooler she could carry, then texted Ellie. *"Heading your way in a few, need anything?"*

"We're good. You and Hank both coming?"

"Yes."

"Together?"

Joni sighed. Why did everyone always ask that? *"Yes, together."*

"Good! See you soon!"

Her friends were great and she loved Ellie, Hank's sister, but really, did everyone have to keep asking if they were together or not? He'd gone with her to her sister's wedding!

Didn't that mean they were together? Just more than casually together. More than friends with some benefits! Why couldn't people accept that? She sighed and texted Hank. *"You ready?"*

"Come over anytime," he texted back.

Joni plastered on her sweet, happy, charming teacher smile, gathered her things getting ready to go out the back door and across the yard to be the best girlfriend ever.

No problems here, No issues. Four more days! She had this! And her floors would look amazing, no doubt.

Putting her phone and keys in her pocket, she picked up her salad, and made sure she locked the door behind her as she left. Walking over to Hank's she smiled again. This would be a great night. No worries at all, she and Hank would have a good time and come home one day closer to her seven day bet. She would so win this one. With perfect Hank, it was hard to win one. He always won. Except sometimes in cornhole, and of course, this time! She had this.

She knocked on his kitchen door and walked in. "I'm here!"

"I am too," he said, standing in the kitchen looking as hot as always in his jeans and sweatshirt and sneakers. It didn't matter what he wore, he was just, well, she hated to say it, perfect.

"Then, let's go," she said. "I texted your sister and she said she didn't need anything, so we are good to go."

He smiled at her in a way that made her want to melt. "I'm ready. Any idea what is on the agenda tonight?"

"Not really. Food, I guess. Getting too cold and windy to play basketball or volleyball. Maybe a game of some kind. Whatever." She flashed him her brightest smile. "We will be together and it will be fun!"

"That's right." He kissed her and then picked up a small box of whatever it was he was bringing. "Let's head out, then."

They went outside and got in his truck, him managing to open the door for her while holding his box. "Seatbelt," he reminded her as he put it in the back seat.

Joni almost snapped back at him but reminded herself she was strawberries and cream tonight, sweet and easy. "Yes, Daddy," she said. "I'm a good girl."

Grinning she heard him snort laugh, as she clicked it in place.

"Good girl, huh?" he said as he got in the driver's seat. "We'll see about that."

"I am!" she insisted, settling the little cooler and her purse between her feet. "Unless you provoke me."

"I am not responsible for your behavior," he said.

"Then why do you think you get to spank me, if you aren't responsible?"

"Because I'm the one with the paddle and you're the one who has the cute butt and the attitude."

"I don't have an attitude," she said, as civilly as she could. What was wrong with him?

"Joni, babe, we've already discussed this. Do you really want to do it again?"

Yeah, she really did. "No."

"That's good. You already agreed and I already have a buffer rented for the weekend."

"What?"

"Well, one of us will be buffing, right? I'm just getting ready."

"See," she said, trying not to feel annoyed. "Perfect."

Hank shook his head. "No one is perfect, Joni. Not even me."

"You are close enough to be very annoying," she informed him.

"Sorry about that," he said in a way that she knew meant he wasn't sorry at all.

Ellie and Mike lived about ten minutes out of town, down a picturesque country lane. It started to rain halfway there, and she smiled. There was something very comforting about being in Hank's truck in the rain with him driving. As he did everything, he drove very well, safely, confidently and she never worried with him behind the wheel, even in the worst of conditions. This was just a gusty fall rain, nothing more, and he didn't even seem to notice. She watched the rain coming down through the trees lining the road to the house, as always, she vowed to figure out what Mike really did for a living. She knew he did some kind of investing, but their house was beyond gorgeous, way more than Ellie's city manager job could afford. Or two teachers, for that matter, she looked over at Hank, wondering if they got together, where would they live? She loved her Grandma's house and had worked hard the last few years making it her own. Could she move out of it? Probably, but into his house? Yeah, that would be challenging for her. He was always remodeling and renovating and he was so particular about even the little things. There was a proper way to do things and that was his way.

"Almost there," he said.

"Really? I didn't notice," she said, too quickly, then bit her lip. Strawberries and cream, she reminded herself. "Yeah, there's their lane."

"I'm going to drop you at the front door. Looks like they have a houseful already."

"You don't have to do that," she said, gathering her purse and cooler, knowing he would anyway.

"I know, but I'm all sweet like that." He smiled at her and she couldn't help but smile back. The man was just handsome.

"Thank you," she told him, actually glad she didn't have to run through the rain like he would. Sometimes it was good to be female. "Want me to take your box, too?"

"I have it well covered, I got it," he said, pulling around

the cars parked alongside the long circle driveway up to the front door and unlocking the car door. Then he reached into the back seat and pulled out a large cowboy hat and plopped it on her head "There, now you won't get your pretty hair all wet. See you in a minute."

She thought about protesting, like, what about his pretty hair? But, remembering not to sweat the small stuff tonight, climbed out, dashing to the door. Standing under the covered portico, she rang the bell, which Ellie answered right away.

"Joni! I'm glad you're here!" she said. "Where's my brother?"

"Parking the truck," she said. "He'll be right behind me."

Joni noted her little friend had what seemed to be red rimmed eyes. Was she all right? She'd have to ask her later, but Hank came running up behind her and she moved out of his way.

He barely looked damp, which was annoying. If she ran through that downpour, especially without a hat, she'd look like a drowned rat. He smiled at Ellie. "Hey, baby sister."

"Hey, big brother," she said. "Wipe your feet, Henry and give me that box of whatever yummy stuff you made. The guys are in the den attempting to start a fire."

"Sounds good," he said after diligently wiping his feet, and strode toward the back of the house.

"Come on, Joni," Ellie said, and Joanie followed her to where she already heard laughter in the air. She sighed happily, a night out with her friends was just what she needed tonight. Away from all the angst that was Hank and his perfection. Well, he's here, but she wouldn't be interacting with only him. Her friends would be a buffer, and when they got home later, she'd be one day closer to having gorgeous floors.

"Joni!" she heard.

She smiled as she put the fruit salad down on the counter and hugged her friends. Lucy, as always, was flitting about doing her Lucy thing. Jordyn was there, looking laid back as always. Hopefully she brought something wonderful from her bakery.

"Is this all of us or are you expecting more?" she asked Ellie.

"I invited Izzy and Shana, but they couldn't make it, so it's just the eight of us. Hear anything more from Beth?"

Joni smiled. "She's doing great. Loves life over in Zephyrhills and being married. He treats her well and I know he will take care of her." Her mind flashed to the thought of Beth's bedroom door standing open. When she knew it had been closed when she left for work. Her house was equipped with all the latest security gizmos and gadgets, though, so she wasn't really concerned, except, well, she was, a little. Her little sister had an ex-boyfriend turned abuser turned stalker and while they had moved out of town, he'd found them and moved there too, which apparently was just fine with law enforcement. But now, Beth was safely ensconced in a different state with a new family who would protect her. The man was still in town and Joni wondered if he was searching for Beth in their house. No way could he get through all their security, though. She shook her head and took the glass of wine Ellie offered her. No worries tonight. Tonight was for friends who were like family.

"How's business, Jordyn?" she asked.

Jordyn smiled. "Can you believe holiday orders are already coming? And I have three – count them three – December brides to bake for!"

"Wow, that's a lot of cake," Joni said. "School gets out December twelfth for Christmas break, if you need an extra part time hand, I'd love to help out."

"I'll count on you," Jordyn said, then turned to Lucy. "Moriah has been asking about coming on full time. I'm considering it, what do you think?"

Lucy flipped her pink streaked hair back from her face. "You know Moriah doesn't listen to anything I say. I mean, I'm just the big sister, why would she? Is she not nannying for Heidi anymore? What about school?"

"I'm not sure," Jordyn said. "I know she's still living with Heidi, but she's coming in next week, so I'll find out all the details."

"Well, let me know. I worry about her."

"She's doing great, Lucy. At least from what I can tell," Jordyn said, "But of course I'll let you know."

Lucy sighed and picked up a cupcake. "She makes me want to ruin my dinner!" she said dramatically.

"Wow! That would teach her," Joni laughed, but empathized with Lucy. She knew how hard it was to be watching over a little sister and worrying and not being able to do anything about it. Moriah and Lucy had both escaped a background she didn't know much about and figured she probably didn't want to know. Lucy had lived with Ellie and her grandma for a while, growing up, and then a few years later, Lucy had rescued a runaway Moriah. They both were thriving and doing well, but she knew Lucy worried about the rest of her siblings still trapped in what sounded like a cult like environment.

"What can I do to help, Ellie?" she asked, putting her glass down and going to the sink to wash some dishes. She heard the men heading their way and reminded herself, strawberries and cream. She had this.

Chapter 3

"Did you have a good time?" Hank asked her as she climbed in the truck a few hours later.

"I did! How about you?"

"What is it with Lucy and her idea that we like to play kids' board games?"

Joni laughed. "Lucy didn't get to play much as a kid. I think she's catching up on her childhood."

"I'm around kids all day. I don't need to relive my youth." He put the truck in gear and they headed down the drive. The rain had softened to a gentle mist and it seemed so romantic in the dark, driving along the road with only the sound of the wipers' gentle rhythm.

"You're just upset because you didn't win," she teased him.

"Yeah, I know." He flashed her a grin. "Silly, huh?"

"Little bit." She held her fingers up to show him how small. He grabbed her hand and kissed her fingers which made her smile. "But on the plus side, you didn't irritate me much at all!"

"We aren't home yet," he said and seemed to be in a better mood. "I still can't believe I can't win at Monopoly."

"You can. You just didn't today," she said.

"Yeah, I guess that is right," he said. "We will have to have a rematch."

"Strip Monopoly?" she said. "In front of the fire? Sounds romantic."

"Nah, you'd have an unfair advantage. You'd be naked and I'd be distracted."

"But you'd be winning," she said, feeling in a good mood. Dinner had been delicious as always when Ellie and Mike cooked and they all got together. Ellie's new house was simply made for entertaining. She'd planned it that way, with all her committee meetings she held there.

"I would be, in more ways than one." He let go of her hand and patted her leg. "Naked you in front of the fire, and me deservedly winning. Sounds like a plan."

"Aww, you say the sweetest things," she told him.

"I know, it's a gift," he said smugly and she looked at the clock on the dash. Another twenty minutes, he could drop her off at her house and she'd be safe for another day. It was like he wasn't even trying! That wasn't like him at all. He knew how to wind her up from zero to sixty in less than a minute. Why wasn't he making an effort so she could show him how nothing he said bothered her and she was all strawberries and cream? Well, it didn't matter. As long as she won the bet. And she was going to. So why she went off on him less than five minutes later boggled her mind. This was not supposed to happen. All he did was ask her about her alarm system.

"It is working. I keep it updated and checked out. Besides, no one is after me, you know."

"Sociopaths don't make sense," he said. "If he can't find his target, he could easily come after you to find out where she is."

She felt annoyed, knowing he had checked the system out himself more than once. He seemed to know as much as any of the alarm techs who came out and of course, now he seemed to think it was his job to do it. It wasn't! He was her boyfriend, not her bodyguard. She didn't need a bodyguard.

"Hank, I'm fine! I wish you'd stop fussing at me!"

"No, you don't," he said, not taking his eyes off the road. "You like knowing I care."

"That isn't true! Well, it's true but I don't need a daddy! I'm a grown up!"

"You think?" he said, and she saw that annoying grin sneak over his face. What was so funny?

"Pretty sure." She tried to keep her temper under control. "Why are you so interested in my alarm system all of a sudden?"

"I just worry about you there alone," he said. "It's what men do. Take care of their females. Not because they can't take care of themselves, but because they are important."

"Yeah, I saw that meme too," she said, trying to keep her temper. "But protecting me does not need to include asking me repeatedly about my alarm system."

"Fine," he said, and turned the truck down their street. "I went over the other day and it wasn't on."

"What?" Okay that wasn't true.

"Yes, I went over to fix that leak in your bathroom sink and the alarm wasn't on."

"You fixed my sink and didn't tell me? When?"

"The other day when you were out grocery shopping. But the alarm wasn't on. That's the point, not the sink."

"No one asked you to come willy nilly and fix stuff!" Why was her voice rising? Strawberries and cream, she reminded herself. Was that the day Beth's bedroom door was open?

"Willy nilly?" He threw her a look. "And you are welcome, by the way. And the alarm wasn't on."

"Was too! It's automatic anyway. I always set the alarm."

"Joni, it wasn't. That's why I've been bringing it up. Beth's only been gone a little while and you're already slacking off on safety and that just isn't smart."

"So now, I'm not smart?" Yeah, there went her voice again. Why did he do this to her?

"Joni, you know that isn't what I said." He didn't even seem exasperated. Well, she was. Enough for both of them.

"Really, it sounded like it to me." They were only two blocks from home. She could walk the rest of the way. Get away from his annoyingness before she said something she regretted. "I don't know why you do this to me! I did set the alarm and I'm not stupid! And I really resent you saying I am! You may be a genius but we work the same job, you know."

"What does that have to do with anything?" He looked over at her, seemingly baffled and she couldn't take anymore. Why did he do this to her every time? All she needed to do was get out of this truck.

"For the love of all things," she said, feeling so exasperated and mad, she just couldn't deal with him anymore, and when he slowed down to the stop light, she grabbed the door handle to get out.

He did something he'd never done before and her heart sank as she realized what she'd done. He reached over and grabbed her other arm and held onto it. He had always let her go before. Just let her climb out and now, she realized suddenly she'd be buffing floors this weekend. He reached over and child locked her door and then let go of her arm and fished a quarter out of the cup holder. "Hang on to this until we get home," he said. "Then, go straight to the living room by the fireplace. Drop your jeans and panties to your ankles and lift up your shirt so I can see that pretty bottom that's going to have some nice color to it soon. Then quarter to the wall till I tell you to get over my knees. And I expect you to cooperate."

Joni slumped in her seat, and didn't even try messing with the door lock. Yeah. Three days and she already blew it. Had she done it on purpose despite her best effort? Her decision not to test him? Why did she think her answer was a solid maybe? She clutched the quarter in her hand. "I'm sorry," she said as meekly as she could muster. "I don't know what happened."

"Yes, you do," he said. "So you will get to find out." He reached over and patted her knee, almost consolingly. "You will find out I follow through."

Yeah. Well, she had no doubts about that, just about the concept. He drove down their road, and she shivered almost convulsively. "I'm really sorry," she tried again. "I don't know what happened, but really I set the alarm. I know I did and I'm sorry about blowing up."

"Not as sorry as you will be," he replied way too cheerfully, she thought as he pulled into her driveway not a minute later.

Unlocking the child lock he put his hand over hers, curled her hand around the quarter and looked in her eyes. "Now march. Get yourself in there and get ready for me."

"May I go to the bathroom first?" she asked feeling suddenly overwhelmed.

He hesitated just a minute. "You have two minutes. Do what you need to do and I expect to see a bare bottom waiting for your spanking in that corner when I come in."

"Yes, Sir," she said, wondering why she said that. She occasionally called him Daddy when he was being overly protective and dramatic but that was mostly sarcasm, she had never called him Sir. That was what she was concerned about right now? What she was calling him?

He reached back and plopped the hat on her head again to guard against the light rain. "Get to moving. Your two minutes start now."

She hesitated. "Hank?"

"What, baby?"

"It will be okay?" Why wasn't she fighting this?

"It will be. Better start moving."

Grabbing her hat with one hand and her purse with the other, she ran to his house and let herself in with her key. Hurrying to the bathroom, she peeked in the mirror at her bottom. What would her bottom look like later? Surely he didn't mean blisters for real? He couldn't. He, well, was that even possible? Shivering, trembling, she dried her shaking hands, picked the quarter up again, and made her way to the fireplace. Could she do this? Maybe she should make a fire? Maybe she should do as she was told. She felt cold and damp, very nervous and even a little scared. Could she really do this? Shivering again while thinking of what he might do if she wasn't waiting for him, where he wanted her, in the position he wanted her, she looked around the room for a clear wall. Most of the room was filled with bookcases.

He said by the fireplace, so she shuffled over as slowly as she could. Yeah, there was a spot. Clutching the quarter tightly in her hand, she unsnapped her jeans. Was she really doing this? Why was it so hard? She'd dropped her pants in front of him more than once, but that was always for a good time. This was to correct her behavior. She was a grown adult! She didn't need her behavior corrected! Would this correct it, she wondered. After the next few minutes would no one ever ask again if they were together or not? Somehow she doubted it, but who knew? She guessed she'd find out.

She heard the back door open and close and hurried to the wall, she dropped her jeans but they only fell to her knees. She couldn't bear the idea of pulling her panties down to match, though. However, she did put the quarter against the wall and pushed her nose against it. What was this supposed to do again? Oh, yeah, give her time to calm down and reflect. Was she? No. She was trying to hold the stupid coin up and trying not to wiggle with nerves and listening for him and…"So where is the bare bottom I wanted to see?" Oh there he was.

Her body almost convulsed with nerves and anticipation. "I can't," she whispered.

"Try," he suggested. "By the time I count to five. One. Two."

"I am! I am! Wait!" What was he going to do if she didn't? Spank her? But she suddenly felt the need to do as she was told and wiggled while trying to hold the quarter against the wall. "See!" Her pants fell to her ankles.

"Panties too. I need a good target to get that little bottom nice and red," he said and she choked back an almost sob.

Could she? Slowly, she put her fingers in her waistband and pulled them down to her thighs. They weren't going to fall off like her jeans did, though and she couldn't move because her nose made her immobile. However, despite her trembling fingers, she managed to shove them halfway down her thighs.

"Lift the shirt." She heard from behind her. "I need to see that naughty bottom."

Joni thought about protesting that her bottom had done nothing naughty but decided that discretion was the better idea at this point in time and reached back to lift her shirt up, exposing herself. She'd never felt as naked as she did in this moment in time. And she really wasn't. But she felt that way, a lot. It was humiliating to stand there with the quarter against her nose and one hand holding up her shirt behind her back to show him what he wanted to see, her bare bottom, waiting to be spanked.

"Not bad for a first try. We'll work on technique next time," he said and her heart sank. Next time? Wasn't this a one and done and man, she'd forgotten all about the floor buffing she now owed him. Fun weekend ahead. She wiggled, trying not to drop the quarter. Would she even be able to sit down to teach tomorrow? How bad was this going to be?

She could hear him next to her and again tried not to wiggle. "Are you thinking how smart it was to have a little tantrum in the truck?" he asked her. She almost shook her head, but stopped, as she heard him moving logs around to start a fire but didn't dare look. What would he do if she dropped the quarter?

"I didn't," she started, almost automatically. That's what she was supposed to be doing, right? Contemplating her sins? Instead her mind was racing with thoughts. She should act as if she was, at least. "Yes. I mean no. It wasn't smart."

"Raise your shirt higher," he said. "Your bottom needs the cool breeze because in a minute it's going to get a little warm."

"You don't have to–" she said, trying not to feel desperate and she really needed to pee again, but that was probably just nerves.

"You'd be disappointed in me if I didn't. I don't want to fail the test." She felt more than saw him stand up and away from the fire with her nose firmly plastered to the wall. It did not itch. "Shirt, higher. Now."

Joni gave a small whimper but again, did as she was told. Was she ever going through this again? Nope. No matter what. Why had she agreed to this? And she had. She knew she did. And, she reminded herself, this was the easy part. Next step would be placing herself across his knees and accepting her spanking. That would be worse. She should be grateful for the time in the corner, but she wasn't. Her nose itched now, and she didn't like standing still for so long, and she hated holding her shirt up, showing him, well, what he wanted to see. How long was she going to stand here? Half of her wanted to be done with it, and just get it over with and the other half thought standing here forever would be just fine. Next time, if there were ever a next time which there wouldn't be, would be worse because she would know what was coming.

"You ready?" he finally asked her a hundred-million minutes later.

"No," she said, truthfully.

"Too bad. Kick the pants and panties off and get over here."

Swallowing hard, Joni dropped her shirt and grabbed the quarter and put it in her hoodie pocket. At least she made a quarter. Unless he wanted it back. She'd see if he asked for it. Oh, yeah, her jeans. She didn't turn around to look at him, but kicked off her shoes, then her jeans and hesitated. He didn't say anything as she pulled her panties down and stepped out of them. Should she pick them up and fold them or leave them puddled on the floor? Luckily, he told her what to do. "Get over here and stand in front of me."

He was sitting on the couch and she wondered if she pulled her shirt off over her head and flashed him if he'd be distracted enough to, well, not do what he was planning to do? But she took a big shaky breath and her feet turned and moved toward him. He sat, settled in the middle of the couch and pointed right between his spread legs. Exhaling loudly she walked over there as slowly as she dared. This would really happen. Was happening. Standing where he pointed, she tried not to squirm, but it was humiliating and she felt so embarrassed. Why was she doing this? She could put on her pants right now and walk out and they both knew it. But no, she was standing in front of him, listening to him lecture her about something. What? Did he really think she could hear him? Pay attention? This was not how she wanted to end the evening. Was it? Maybe it was or she would have controlled her mouth.

"Look at me." Oh, she heard that.

Raising her head, she looked into his gorgeous eyes. They usually sparkled with his mostly good moods and smiles, but these eyes seemed stern and not at all Hank-like. "Now, get over my lap and take your spanking for acting like the naughty girl you are."

She shut her eyes and did as she was told feeling stupid and awkward and, yes, fearful. Lying across his lap felt even more awkward than standing up. 'Scoot up a little more," he said.

What did that even mean? She had stretched out across his lap, and put her head and legs on the couch. But she used her arms and pulled herself up a little. He gave her bottom a pat and she flinched as she heard him say, "That's better. Is my naughty girl ready to be punished?"

Well, no. He smacked her sharply and said, "Answer me. Now."

"Yes, Sir." She assumed that was the right answer but felt proud of herself for not yelping. That stung. Luckily the next couple weren't hard at all, and she relaxed a little. Okay, spankings could be handled. He stopped and rubbed a few times and that made the very slight sting feel almost warm and, well, nice, then he smacked again, a little harder. That was still bearable. She could deal with this. However, she didn't like the idea that he was fully clothed and she was mostly naked but for her hoodie and her socks. "Ow!" Okay, this set was harder than the last. That almost hurt, but he stopped and rubbed again.

"Let's get this bottom nice and warmed up and then we'll start your spanking," he said.

"Start?" Hadn't he already started? Wasn't this her spanking? What did that mean? Again he did another fairly light set of about six and she again relaxed as he rubbed.

"Nice and warm, and you're ready. Now, remember this next time you want to throw yourself a little temper tantrum," he said as she steeled herself for the next round.

"Ow!" she yelped. 'That hurt!"

"That was nothing," he said and she thought she heard a

hint of amusement in his voice. If testing him had been her goal, she was totally done with it now! Timed tests were a thing.

"Was too something!" she said and wiggled, trying to get away from his hand. She grabbed the couch pillow tightly, now wanting to put her hand back to shield her poor bottom. Her hand would probably hurt worse. "Ow! That hurts!" She wiggled again, wondering if she could slide off the couch. "Please?" He kept a steady staccato of spanks and they seemed not to stop. She felt a surge of something rush through her. Adrenaline? Fear? "No more!" she heard her voice rise and hated she was begging. "I'll be good!"

"Oh this little bottom is barely pink," he said. "We have a long way to go, yet."

"No!" she sobbed out. Why had she been curious about this? It was not fun! It was not sexy play, it felt like, well, punishment. "Please! No more. I can't!"

"Yet, I think you can and will," he said. "You misbehaved and need to accept your punishment."

"I can't!" She tried to crawl off his lap. She had to get out and away. "I can't, please!" It seemed he spanked harder at those words, and even while she tried to wiggle and squirm, he had her held tightly against him. She hurt too much to even wonder how. Her legs kicked up, trying to stop his hand from spanking her and her one hand went back to try to stop it. "It hurts! Please!"

That seemed to stop nothing as he continued the repeated smacks while she wiggled and kept trying to get away, off his lap. Down to the floor, over on the side of the couch, something! Her bottom stung and he wasn't stopping to rub the sting out anymore. "I'm sorry! Please no more! Okay, I'm done! Ow ow ow! It hurts! Please!" Why was she begging so pathetically? So loudly? Why not? If he didn't like it, he could stop.

Finally it seemed to be over, though it took a minute for that to sink in, and she felt him rubbing her hot throbbing bottom. "Come here," she heard but she couldn't move, could only lie there and cry. "I said come here." His tone sounded strict and stern and she forced herself off his lap. The easiest thing seemed to be to fall between his knees and put her head on his lap. The tears kept falling and she almost convulsed, sobbing on his leg. Had it hurt that much? Yes! It was horrible! Nothing to like about it at all! How could he do that to her?

"I didn't like that." She looked up at him, knowing she was a mess with her face all red and her nose running, tears still filling her eyes. "It hurt."

"It was supposed to hurt. You were being taught a lesson. Did you learn it?" He seemed concerned that she did. Why?

She nodded but really, couldn't remember what she was supposed to learn.

"Well, tell me," he said, and started smoothing her hair for her.

"I don't know." She took a couple of breaths that still shook.

"What don't you know?"

"I don't know that either!" she wailed and crawled up and onto his lap and into his arms. "I just don't know." Why wouldn't her brain work? Shock? Maybe. Her mild mannered genius boyfriend had resorted to a time honored method of curing behavior. Had it worked? Right now she couldn't even remember what she'd done.

He hugged her tightly and held her close. "Shh, it's okay. You'll calm down in a minute."

Joni shook her head and repeated, while holding him as tightly as she could. "I don't know."

"We've established that," he said. "Maybe next time I should send you back to the corner after your spanking so you can remember."

With that she shook her head harder and pressed herself tighter against him. "Don't send me away," she begged, disliking how powerless she felt and how pathetic she sounded. "And never again!"

"Well, we will see about that. In the meantime, you want to walk upstairs or for me to carry you?"

"Carry, please," she said. Heck with worrying about him ruining his back. That was a him problem, not a her problem. He was the one who made her all shaky, after all.

Chapter 4

Hank stopped raking the mulch into his garden, getting it ready for spring, which would be coming after a looming long Illinois winter. His garden, he dreamed, instead of mulch and dead leaves would be alive with bright colors, blossoms on thickly planted flowers, healthy vegetables and his little grape vine. Wine making was on his list of 'want to learn' projects. Winter had its perks, of course, but Spring was always welcome. He smiled. Although he knew he could make much more money doing something, almost anything, else, he loved Clearwater and he loved the life he'd created here. Money couldn't buy the happiness and the contentment he'd carved into his daily existence. He had plenty for his needs and most of his wants. He could travel in the summers, doing research on his book, had plenty to keep him occupied and his mind thriving. What else was there? Well, his little tantrum thrower over his knee a few more times. She'd responded very well to her correction a few days back. Of course, the aftereffects were fading already, and she had pouted all the way through her floor buffing chore, but had done it. He'd expected her to start acting out again here soon.

She'd be ready for a second punishment before the next week-end, he felt sure.

Speak of the little she-devil, his phone rang her familiar ring and he smiled as he picked it up. "Henry?" she said sounding frantic, totally unlike herself, "We need you."

"Where are you?" he asked. "What's going on?"

"Down at Jordyn's bakery, can you hurry?"

"Be there in just a couple minutes," he said, dropping his rake on the ground. There was something wrong, no doubt. He could tell by her voice. The bakery was only a few blocks away and he could run there faster than he could find his keys, get in his truck and drive. He was concerned but not upset. Yet. Joni rarely called him Henry unless she was upset, and she hated asking for help. Maybe they just needed him to change a light bulb or something, he thought, setting out at a fast jog. No, Jordyn's fiancé Ben was much handier than he was, so it probably wasn't anything like that. His brain buzzed but it only took a few minutes to get there, and he was met at the door by Joni, who threw herself into his arms, while he gave her a tight hug. Yes, something was wrong and it wasn't a light bulb. When he released her, she relocked the door behind him. "Thank you for coming. You are the smartest person we know, and we don't know what to do."

She looked scared, he noticed. "Jordyn have a break in?" he asked. Joni shook her head.

"Tasting room," she said, heading to the little room off to the side, which oddly had the curtains pulled, closing it off from the main room. He walked into it, with her on his heels and the first thing he saw was Ben with his arm around, was that Miranda? He knew her, of course. He'd run into her at social gatherings, community events and seen her at the diner he frequented. She was always dressed in what he thought of as her power suits. Well-tailored skirts and blazers, no matter the weather and always with her signature high heels that other women seemed to envy for some reason. Today, though, she sat in one of Jordyn's comfortable chairs in jeans and what looked like one of Ben's flannel shirts, sneakers and the most badly beaten up face he'd ever seen.

Stopping short in the doorway, he looked at Ben and asked, "Eli?" Ben nodded.

"Where is he?"

"Vanished," Jordyn said. "Miranda tried to break up with him and he didn't take that well. She didn't show up at work the other day and one of the contractors called Ben who went over and found her on the floor. She just now got out of the hospital. The police have a BOLO out for him, and an arrest warrant, but he's long gone."

"How did I not hear about this?" Hank asked, pulling Joni around from behind him to his side and pulling her in close.

"No one knew but Ben and I until today. Joni stopped by and found out, and insisted we call you."

"You are the smartest man, I know," Joni said. "You'll know what to do."

Do? What did they mean do? They'd called the cops and Eli, who had terrorized and almost killed Joni's little sister Beth, had done one of his famous vanishing acts. He felt bad that he felt almost glad it was Miranda and not Joni he'd taken his fury out upon. He saw Miranda's black and blue bruised eyes filling with tears.

"I can't stay here," she said. "I can't." Her voice was hoarse as if she'd been screaming for days and he winced. That big, oversized shirt probably covered up a lot of bruises and probably some broken ribs.

"I told her about him coming into my house," Joni said, sounding almost hysterical.

"He what?" This was very sudden unwelcome news. "You didn't tell me that."

She looked down at the floor but her voice rose and it was

easy to feel her fear "I think so. I can't prove it, but I've come home three times now to Beth's bedroom door opened and the last two times, things were moved around. Then the other day," she hesitated and looked at him. "There was this jar of olives in the fridge. I hate them. But they are Beth's favorite. They were not there before."

"Did you call the cops?" he asked, almost forgetting Miranda in his sudden panic. "Look at the security tapes?"

"I looked at them but nothing was on there. Nothing. I couldn't call the cops and tell them a door was open and there were olives in my refrigerator."

"You could have told me," he said.

She shrugged and looked at Miranda. "What do we do? She's scared and is afraid he will come back and finish the... her... well, you know."

"She's staying with me for now," Ben said, "but she wants to vanish, move somewhere else. Start over. I've moved before, but I left a forwarding address and all that. I'm just a handyman. I don't know what to do. How to help her."

"So we called you," Joni said. "You know things."

Yeah, he knew things. Like once she calmed down, she was going straight over his knee and she'd remember to tell him important things. Like someone was breaking into her house!

"Miranda," he looked straight at the battered woman, someone he'd never really cared for much, and said with as much empathy as he could put in his voice, "I'm so sorry this happened to you. I'll do my best to help you. Give me a little time, okay?"

She nodded. "Thank you," she said, her voice barely a whisper.

"Ben, can I talk to you for a minute?" Hank asked.

"Sure," he said, looking at his sister. "You stay here with Joni and Jordyn and I'll be back in a minute and will take you home, okay?"

"I can't go home!" her voice rose and Hank winced. She was terrified, it was obvious.

"My home, little sister. I'm not letting you out of my sight. I'll keep you safe."

She nodded and Hank saw Jordyn and Joni move closer to her as Ben got up and walked to the door. Hank stepped back and they walked out to the larger room, out of eyesight and earshot.

"I'm sorry to drag you into this," Ben said. "I'm just at a loss. I don't know what to do to help her."

"I have a couple ideas," Hank said. "I know a safe place, but need to make some arrangements first."

"I'm so mad, too," Ben said. "All I want to do, is—" He made a motion with his hand that Hank understood.

"You have help now," he told him. "Just keep her safe for the next few days and I'll see what I can come up with. He's a coward, you know. He's long gone."

"Yeah, but he'll show back up again. He's like Teflon. You know how he got away with what he did to Beth."

"I know," Hank said, feeling impotent. He could only imagine how Ben felt. "I'll call in some favors, okay, and then I'll get back to you in the next couple of days." In the meantime, he had a little lady of his own who needed some reminders of how to behave and what things were important to tell him.

They walked back into the tasting room and he saw Ben try to smile at his sister. If something like that had happened to his sister Ellie, he didn't know what he'd do. Yeah, he knew exactly what he'd do. What was wrong with that evil son of a bitch? He swallowed hard. He did not want to even think about that.

"Miranda, don't worry. I'm figuring something out. You just stay with Ben and try to heal, rest up, okay? Do what the doctors told you to do. I'll be in touch in a few days." She nodded and he saw the tears rolling down her face again. Poor thing. He hoped he could follow through and help her. He hoped what he thought was true, actually was, and they would rally around.

First he would deal with this one. Then he'd make that phone call.

"Joni, come on, let's go home," he said, glad he hadn't driven over. She had her car here though, he'd seen it outside when he came in. She said a few words to Jordyn and Miranda and stood up and walked out under his arm and through the door. He had an intense desire to smack her butt but reminded himself he was the calm one. He'd cool off and then give her a reason to remember to tell him about things like an insane stalker breaking into her house. He knew it was him as well as she did. Why hadn't she told him? He'd be finding out. After what he did to her sister and now to Miranda, he was going to make sure she told him even if she saw a shadow that looked out of place.

"Are you okay?" he asked as she handed him her keys.

She shook her pretty head and whispered, "Not really. I keep seeing Beth in my mind. Finding her on the floor. I can't imagine."

"How did you happen to find out about this mess?" he asked, opening her car door.

"I told Jordyn I'd stop by with some college financial aid information I was leaving for Moriah, who is working there tomorrow, and then forgot, so came after she closed. She gave me a key a while back in case she got locked out, because I live the closest, and since I didn't see any lights on, I just unlocked the door and walked in. I was just going to put it on the counter for Moriah. They had just checked Miranda out of the hospital and were all back in the tasting room and didn't have any choice but to tell me. Besides, with my involvement with, well, Beth, like I said, they didn't have any choice. They had to tell me."

"And yet, you didn't have to tell me about your break ins?" He could tell immediately she felt guilty.

"I didn't know they were, for sure! There was nothing on the camera!" That was a defensive tone if he ever heard one.

"Yeah. Cameras can never be hacked, or turned off. That just isn't a thing."

"Sarcastic much?" she mumbled. "I didn't know for sure and didn't want to bother you. I didn't want you to think I was crazy."

He pulled into her driveway and turned to look at her. "Bother me? With a madman after your family and in your house, and you didn't want to bother me?" His hand shook as he reached into her change holder between them. He didn't care what he pulled out. A penny, dime or quarter. "Get your ass in the kitchen and it better be in the corner and bare and don't you even think about disobeying me."

She snatched the coin from his hand and he watched her flee into the kitchen. He had to calm down. He could not administer her punishment while he was so shaken up. Just seeing Miranda, and knowing what Ben was going through, he could be going through too. He picked up his phone and called his brother-in-law. "Mike"

"Hank, what's wrong?"

How did he know? Did it matter? "Eli recently attacked Miranda and has supposedly left town. However, can you keep an eye on Ellie? Just put her on a leash and keep her close for a while. Just in case he goes around looking, well, I know it's a stretch but, she's my baby sister."

"Was it bad?" Mike asked.

"Yes. I'm keeping Joni with me for a few days at least and I'll call Nick and warn him a little later tonight. I hope the scumbag doesn't know where Beth is, but he knows Joni knows and that I probably do. So—"

"So, Ellie," Mike said. "No problem. Let me know what I can do to help if anything. You know Miranda and I have a past too, and he's probably heard about it."

"I did know that," Hank admitted. "Another reason to take care of my little sister."

"We need this solved, Hank," Mike told him. As if he didn't know.

"I realize that," he said. "I have an ace up my sleeve. I'm going to see if it works out. I think it will, but until then. Ellie."

"I will protect her with my life, even if it means chaining her to the bed."

Hank smiled for the first time in a few hours. "That might be a little drastic."

"Have you not met your hard-headed sister?"

"A few times. Thanks, Mike. I'll keep you updated."

"Appreciate it. Talk soon."

They hung up and Hank took a deep breath. Time to go remind Joni of what was important. He hoped she had done what she was told because he wasn't in the mood to coddle her tonight. Tonight she needed to learn what he was teaching.

He reminded himself to be calm. This was a lesson, a correction for her, not a fear based reaction for him, he reminded himself. Cool heads and all that.

Taking another deep breath, he walked into the kitchen where she had gone and noticed she had done as she had been told, but her slender shoulders were shaking. He knew she was crying, and he didn't blame her. Her pants and panties were both at her ankles and her sweater wasn't long enough to cover her bare bottom. He'd left her waiting long enough, but reached over and grabbed a wooden spoon from the utensil holder. That would get his point across. He almost smiled as he went over to the table and pulled out a chair, but he didn't know why.

"Get your bare butt over my lap now," he said. He tried not to growl but it wasn't coming out right. How dare she put herself at risk, not tell him? Even put her sister at risk. There had to be something in the house that said where Beth was. He briefly thought of Joni's mom and her other sister Sydney and made a mental note to have Joni call them. After he was done.

She shuffled over to him, her face looking so sad and upset, he only wanted to take her in his arms and comfort her. That time would come. Now was the time to enforce his rules, for her safety.

"Get yourself over my lap," he commanded. She stopped and looked in his eyes, hers already tear filled. He tried to harden his heart. This lesson she had to learn, for her own safety.

He took a deep breath to calm himself as she, very reluctantly it seemed, draped herself over his knee, head dangling and feet on the floor, hands bracing herself. "So start explaining," he smacked her bottom, a little too hard and she gave what sounded like an involuntary yelp.

"I wasn't sure," she started. He smacked her again.

"You were sure enough," he said. And gave her two more fairly hard smacks. "Why didn't you say anything?"

Stubbornly, she didn't answer him, so he smacked her already pink-colored bottom four more times, spreading the wealth between both cheeks. He wanted her to remember this tomorrow. Maybe the next day. "Answer me."

"I don't know," she wailed.

"Start thinking then." He gripped the wooden spoon and made sure he aimed right for the middle four more times. That made her howl a little. Good.

"I'm sorry!" That didn't even deserve a response, so he

peppered her little bottom while she began wiggling and her feet came up off the floor. He didn't care, she could kick all she wanted. The visual was rather cute and it didn't hinder his spanking ability any. He could handle any little tricks she had to try and stop him.

He heard a few sobs from her and gave one more hard smack. "Well, you ready to talk?"

"Yes!"

"Good." He smacked her once more on her sit spot, just because he could. "Then let's hear it."

Her voice was fairly muffled from below him as she started. "I was just, well, at first I thought I wasn't sure, and then I was, but then I just kept thinking I was crazy, and then I kinda knew but I didn't want to know," she kept blabbering on between her hitching breaths and sniffles. So basically, she was thinking ignore it and it will go away, was what he figured. That was unacceptable.

He finally interrupted her stream of blather and said, "So, you made the decision to put yourself in danger rather than confide in me?"

"No! I mean, I guess, I don't know!"

He'd had enough. He raised the spoon and brought it down hard enough to make her howl loudly. He'd finish up her spanking, making sure she wouldn't forget. "You will always tell me things. You will never lie by omission. You will not put yourself in danger. Do you understand me?" Every word he punctuated with two very firm smacks, one to each reddening cheek. He doubted she could hear him, over her sobs and her frantic efforts to wiggle away from him. However, maybe it was sinking in subconsciously. Or he'd remind her later when her feet weren't kicking and her hands weren't flying back and she wasn't wiggling quite so frantically. Besides, her shrieking overcame his voice anyway.

Finally, he reached down and grabbed an arm to stand her

up in front of him and noticed her frantically start to rub her bottom, so he grabbed both her hands and half enjoyed the wiggles as she tried to dance the sting and burn away. It needed to sink in. "Stand still."

"I can't!"

"You can or you will go back over my knee for more."

She stopped rising on her toes and gyrating and seemed to attempt to control her sobs. "If you ever, ever, see anything out of place again, even see a shadow on a wall, I don't care, you pick up that phone and you call me. Do you understand?" She nodded sniffling, but he said, "Tell me."

"Yes, Sir, I understand."

"Good. Take your hot little bottom and march yourself up to bed." He noticed her eyes flying to the clock. "I don't care what time it is, you get yourself in bed and you stay there." He relented a little when he saw her start crying again. "I'll be up in a little while, and you'll be okay." He kissed her forehead. "Lesson learned?"

She nodded while she wiped her eyes and whimpered. "Okay, then scoot up to bed. Might as well be naked when I get there."

"Yes, Sir," she said so meekly, he had to pull her in for a hug, and hold her tightly. Then he kissed the top of her head while she sobbed in his arms.

"I'm sorry. I just, I don't know, I'm just sorry. I will tell you if I see a shadow out of place, I promise!" Her voice was so teary and sad, he held her tighter. At least she understood he was there to keep her safe.

"You are my good girl, and I know you won't forget again. I love you, you know."

"I love you, too," she whispered and nestled her head into his chest, making a surge of protectiveness overwhelm him.

He hugged her tighter once more, then patted her hot little bottom. "Now head on up. I have a couple phone calls to make and I'll be there to join you, okay? Things will be fine. I'll hold you all night, I promise."

Out of the corner of his eye, he noted her pants and panties on the floor where she'd kicked them off. He'd have to grab them when he went up.

She nodded and he released her hands and saw them fly behind her, and start rubbing her adorably red bottom as she turned to leave the kitchen. She was the cutest little thing, with her sniffles and rubbing her hot bottom. Whoever would have thought he'd find that endearing? But he did, and felt overly protective of his girl as she rubbed her way out of the room and he heard her footsteps on the stairs, doing as she was told. He felt an overwhelming surge of love and protectiveness and knew he would do anything to take care of her, including making her butt red and her nose run.

He oddly, felt better. He wasn't furious with her anymore, she'd been well chastened and had learned her lesson. That was the important thing. His great fear that she would be hurt had dissipated a little. She wouldn't pull a stunt like that again, he felt certain.

He walked over to where he'd laid his phone down earlier and scrolled down till he found the number he wanted.

"Nick, It's Hank. We have a problem."

"Eli," his almost brother-in-law said.

"Yeah. And Miranda."

"Did he kill her?" Hank felt a chill that that was Nick's first thought.

"No. Beat the hell out of her though and skipped town."

"I'm glad she's okay, and no clue where he is?"

"Not one, but the law is on it. Nick, here's the issue. Miranda's terrified and wanting to move. I'm thinking the best place would be to send her to the clan."

There was silence on the other end of the phone while

Hank waited it out. Finally he heard a very tentative, "I don't understand."

"Yes, you do and so do I. I'm far from stupid and I spent a week there, around you and your family. I know you will take care of her. It's what you do. Can you arrange that for me? And, needless to say, your secret is safe with me."

After another long silence Nick said, "I'll ask around. Call me in a day or two. Is she safe till then?"

"Yeah, she's staying with Ben for now, but he can't protect her forever."

"I understand. Okay, Hank. And man," he heard Nick's voice change, lighten up some, "we're going to have to work on our discretion."

"Don't sweat it. Few people are as smart as I am." Hank laughed. "Give Beth a hug from me and we'll talk in a few days."

"Take care of Joni," Nick said.

"Will do. No worries there." Nick clicked off and put his phone down. Time to head to bed and see if he could provide some aftercare to his well chastised girl. He shook his head as he headed upstairs. Who thought he, of all people, would resort to what he just did? Sometimes the old ways worked best though.

Chapter 5

J oni looked around her house. Did she feel safe in here? It had been over a week since she'd found out about what Eli had done. Hank checked in with his sheriff buddy often but there had been nothing from him. It was as if he'd vanished off the planet, but she knew he hadn't. He was lurking around somewhere. He'd be found, eventually, and surely wouldn't dare come back here. She'd talked to Beth every day who assured her she was safe, and there was always someone with her. That almost made Joni smile. When Beth had lived here, she was often alone more than eighteen hours of the day. Now it sounded as if married life and Zephyrhills agreed with her, very much. She sounded happy and not afraid, and that was all that mattered.

She'd been staying with Hank the last few days, while the gossip flew around their little group as well as the entire town. Miranda had made quite a splash here, the year or so she'd lived here. Most people knew her or of her, and her work was in evidence all over town, from houses like Ellie's to Jordyn's bakery, to the new fancy seafood place on the edge of town, even the gift shop at their little zoo. Plus there was that new

BnB on the edge of town she was in the middle of renovating and now, she'd suddenly left. Rumors flew everywhere. Some were wild, that she and Eli had embezzled money and run off together, and others more mundane, she'd been offered a new job and abruptly took it.

Now, however, things were starting to settle down a little, and she would spend the night in her own house tonight and then drive herself to work in the morning. She had to admit, she was a little concerned, but not worried. Her alarms were on, and she knew Hank would be checking on her off and on all night, plus he'd arranged a police drive by. He was very thoughtful and took very good care of her, she admitted to herself. Even if that care involved a very sore rear now and then.

Why did he feel the need to do that? She had to admit their relationship had gotten closer in the last little while since he'd started implementing what he called The Routine. There was nothing routine about it! This was a routine. Checking that everything was locked, that the alarms were on, the doors she'd left open were still open and the ones she closed were still closed. Pulling the curtains, and finding her book to take to bed. Checking that her work for tomorrow was on the table. Brushing her teeth. Those things were a routine, not holding a quarter against the wall with her pants and panties at her ankles and then going over his lap while he lectured her and then made her cry. However, weirdly, it did make her feel closer to him, and that she could rely on him. Why?

Why was the million-dollar question, she thought, as she pulled her quilt down and settled into her bed, which seemed lonely and huge without Hank. It had been really nice sleeping with him the past week. He was a snuggle bug in bed, a sweet, gentle and very thorough lover, and always had warm feet. He even took very good care of her when she had a bad dream, which she'd been having again since Miranda. In fact, she was under strict orders to call him, no matter the time, if she had one tonight. She doubted she would though. He needed his sleep, which is one reason she came home tonight.

Another reason was she needed to think without his distracting presence. When he was around, she felt constantly aware of him. Like a pesky fly who had gotten into the house, and kept buzzing your nose. No, not really. He was much more exciting than a fly. But just as distracting. It was simply hard to think straight when he was near, and recently, it was even harder. Why did having a sore bottom equal to more feelings toward the man who did it? It made no sense at all. She wasn't sure why, but that seemed to be the way it worked. Why? Her mind seemed to be going in circles.

Getting up to make herself a cup of chamomile tea seemed like too much work, so she sighed and settled down into her pillow. She had school in the morning. She needed to sleep. Drifting off, she wondered how Beth was doing and where Miranda ended up. Somewhere safe, she hoped. Hank told her he wasn't going to tell her because the fewer people who knew, the better. She also hoped Eli would get caught soon and this nightmare would be over.

Joni stopped by Jordyn's bakery. She was just buying pastry, she told herself, nothing more. It had been a couple weeks since what she called The Occurrence happened. Gossip about Miranda had died down. One of her assistants had stepped in to finish up the BnB out at the lake. It was as if she had never existed, well, except for when people saw Ben and asked politely about her. He never said more than, "She's doing fine," leaving people to wonder even more, until they didn't. Attention spans, Joni knew, were short, and honestly, while they admired her work, no one really liked Miranda much, even though Ben was well liked. Ben was everyone's friend, volunteered his time for people in need and just was a decent guy. Miranda was a little, well, she always acted as if she were above everyone else. She was royalty and they were peasants. There was this way she had of giving you a compliment wrapped in an insult. *"Oh that dress looks so much better on you than the one you wore the other day."* That kind of thing that you never quite knew how she meant it to be taken.

"Hello, Moriah," she said, seeing Lucy's little sister behind the counter. Her little sister who towered over her big sister by almost half a foot. She was gorgeous, Joni thought, with an almost pang of envy. She felt very mousy and bland next to the tall, willowy, red head.

"Hi, Joni!" she said, smiling, which of course, even enhanced her beauty. "Are you looking for Jordyn? She and Ben are out at the BnB. He wanted her to have a little break and since it's only an hour till we close," she shrugged. "I'm good here."

"I actually came by for those," she said pointing to some filled pastries on the corner. "But, yes, I always like to see Jordyn."

Moriah packaged up the pastries and handed them to her. "Half price last hour," she said, ringing her up. "Gotta make room for the fresh in the morning."

"Is that a new rule?" Joni asked, handing over her card.

"It isn't a rule, just when we get too many," Moriah handed her back her card. "All set, I'll tell Jordyn you stopped by."

"Thanks, so how is school?" she asked while sticking her card back in her wallet.

"Great. I never knew how much I didn't know. I'm having a blast!"

"I'm so happy for you," Joni said, and headed toward the door. "I'll see you soon!"

"Bye," she heard and walked out the door. To be that young again, starting all over in life with everything new spread in front of you. What would she do differently? She'd always taken so much for granted. She wanted to be a teacher, so she became a teacher. She decided to move to Clearwater and her grandmother's house was waiting as a safe haven for her and her sister. She wanted to meet someone and here came Hank. The Perfect Man. What had she done to earn such an easy life when others struggled? When others hurt, and needed things, when other people, other women, strove and tried and never achieved the nice life she had?

Sighing, she got back in her car and headed toward her house. Her phone rang and she picked it up, putting it on speaker. "Bethie! How are you?"

"I'm doing great! I just had a feeling I should check on you, though."

"I'm fine," she assured her. "Just stopped by Baking Memories and got some of your favorite cream-filled pastries."

"Well, that's just mean," Beth said. "Don't suppose you are up to driving them straight over, are you?"

"Sadly, I have to work tomorrow, so I'll just have to be brave and eat them all myself," Joni gave a martyred sigh.

"Oh, I'm so sorry. Are you sure you are okay, though?"

"I am. Are you sure you are okay?"

"Never been better. I love it here. I wish you'd apply for a job here and live closer to me."

"Maybe sometime," Joni said, "but I need to at least finish out this year at school."

"I know. I just worry about you," Beth said.

"Worry about me?" Joni laughed. "Honey, I'm fine. I always have been." She'd just been thinking of how fine she was, in fact.

"I know. Just, well, just be careful. Okay?"

"I promise, and you be careful too. Nick taking good care of you?"

"Amazing care, and all his family is around, and well, while I can understand why Nick needed to leave here and move to Clearwater for a while, I'm really glad we are here. He seems to be happy to be back, too."

"That makes me happy for you, Beth. I'm so very glad. You deserve happiness. I just pulled in at home. Give me a call later if you want, okay?"

"Will do. Love you, Joni," she said and they hung up.

Joni felt a little niggle of worry. What had Beth worried? She wasn't psychic and never had premonitions or anything. She was probably just thinking of her. Beth, like their younger sister Sydney, often over thought everything. Putting it in the back of her mind, she shivered as she went inside. Resetting the alarm, she looked around. Everything seemed normal, nothing out of place. The refrigerator held nothing she hadn't put in there, and no doors were open or closed. She took a deep breath and felt a little better. Beth's intuition was nothing more than nothing, she felt sure and tried to decide what she wanted for supper. Mac and cheese with tuna and peas sounded good. Then she'd start on some seventh grade research papers she needed to grade. That would be fun.

She put the water on to boil for the pasta and heard her phone ring again. "Ellie!" she said. "How are things?"

"Good, how about with you?"

"Great, just getting ready to have supper and then grade papers. A teacher's life is so thrilling, you know."

"I'm getting my volunteers ready for the Christmas parade this year. You did such a great job lining up the participants last year, I'm hoping you will do it again."

"Mike's letting you do it again?" Jordyn teased. "I thought he was wanting you to cut back on your extras."

"Oh, well, yea, but this is the Christmas parade. You know how important that is to the kids and to the town."

"Sure, I'll do that," she said. "Just give me the details when you get them."

"Will do, thanks!" Ellie hung up, presumably to call her next victim, or volunteer. See, she told herself, she had a life. Her life was here in Clearwater. She didn't need anything more, and who said struggles made you stronger? She was strong. She had nothing to prove to anyone. What was Hank doing tonight, she wondered as she ate in front of the TV later. Did it matter? No. He'd been at school today. He was good, she was good. Life was good. So why was she feeling cynical and so antsy? She didn't know, but did know the answer to final Jeopardy so felt good about that. See. Things were normal.

Taking her plate to the kitchen, she put away the leftovers and decided to take a quick walk around the block to settle her nerves before she started grading papers.

Fall in Illinois was chilly and wet, so she grabbed a lined raincoat and her keys and headed out the front door, making sure to lock it behind her. It wasn't quite dark, mostly dusky, and yes, damp. The streetlights were on though and the air felt crisp and clean as she walked. Despite all the drama and angst of Eli, she felt very safe in Clearwater, something unusual in this day and age she knew. She felt certain there were spots in town that weren't as safe and quiet as this one, but they seemed far away right now, walking in the fairyland of mist and dusk and streetlights dancing. Reaching the end of the block, she turned to make a big square. The neighborhood was quiet this time of night, with people home from work and settling in for dinner with their families to catch up on their days apart. She peeked in one window, seeing a dad putting a baby in a highchair as the mom put food on the table. It looked so Norman Rockwell-ish she almost teared up. Did she want that one day? With Hank?

Did that husband put his wife over his knee and spank her? Or was her Henry the strange male in town? Sure, people on the internet said they did it, and if it was on the internet, it had to be true, right? No. Keyboard warriors were a thing, so was storytelling and fantasy. Sure, a big strong male overpowering you and spanking you, then kissing you till you melted was one fantasy. Reality was different. He didn't overpower. He elicited cooperation. Handed you a quarter and told you to go stand in the corner and you did it. Why? Why was she thinking why so much recently? Then he told you to come and put yourself over his knees which wasn't cute and sexy and fun, but embarrassing and awkward and made you feel stupid. Then all you could picture was your butt and, really, it was probably too big and not cute at all despite what he said, mooning him as he rubbed it.

Then the spanking began and it was nothing like it was on the video where they just lay there like zombies and took it without a whimper or protest. How did they do that? She knew she wiggled like crazy, tried to crawl off his lap, her legs kicked and her arms flailed. She begged without shame and cried and protested and pleaded and then finally, sometimes, ugly cried out of pain and the sheer frustration that she couldn't make him stop. After wasn't him wiping a tear off her cheek with a gentle finger but handing her tissues to mop her face and blow her nose while she either wiggled on his lap or danced in front of him trying to rub out the burn. He spanked much too hard, she decided. There was nothing sexy or fun or enjoyable or hot, well, except for her bottom, about a spanking at all.

So, why, the very next time, he handed her a quarter did she go to the wall and do it all over again instead of pocketing it and heading home or kicking him out? She could stop it at any time, she knew. Well, anytime before it started. So why didn't she? She didn't know. It was a major conundrum in her brain and in her life. Then there was the other issue of why, if he didn't do that horrible thing to her, after a few days, she got antsy and mouthy and irritated with him. It seemed like she actually wanted a spanking and that was the furthest thing from her mind. She never wanted one. So why did she act like she did? Very strange, she told herself, as she walked up her front steps and unlocked the door.

"I'm in the kitchen so don't freak out," she heard Hank call from the back of the house.

"I don't freak out," she called back, hanging up her coat and shivering just a little. Her heart seemed to pick up its beat more than it did on her walk. Maybe she didn't have to do cardio? Just have Hank pop in and get her all excited. That would save her some time and effort. She walked to the back of the house and saw him sitting at her table, all handsome, arms folded, and smiling. She grinned at him, feeling like a besotted fool. What was with him? He just made her as crazy happy as he made her crazy irritated.

"Let's go have some fun," he said.

Weirdly, she felt annoyed that he didn't seem worried about where she was or what she was doing. Why didn't he ask?

"What kind of fun?" Now she was irked. He should have been worried about her! Asked her where she'd been. Scolded her for being alone in the dark. Why wasn't he?

"I thought we could go catch the last high school band concert of the season on the square. I heard there will be hot chocolate and donuts and maybe if you are good, I'll go up front and sing along."

Joni felt herself melt. "So help me, Hank, if you sing as well as you do everything else, I'm going to smack you."

"I'm the only one doing any smacking around here, and

from now on, if you want to go for a walk in the dark you could text me, you know." He uncrossed his arms and stood up.

"How did you know I went for a walk?"

"I put an app on your phone," he said as if that were a normal thing to do.

"What does that even mean?" she asked him. She'd heard of those apps where you could track people and locate them. "How do I not know you did this?"

He shrugged. "You were asleep, so I grabbed your phone and added it. Now I don't have to worry about not being able to find you."

"I am not sure how I feel about this," she said. She really wasn't. Did she care he tracked her? Not really. Did she care he didn't tell her? Yeah, a little bit. "How would you like it if I did that to you?"

"Did what to me? Find a way to keep me safe and make sure that some maniac didn't abduct me while still giving me freedom to roam at my will? That?" He cocked his head at her quizzically, looking just adorable.

Joni glared at him. "Your logic is infuriating."

"You are welcome." He smiled at her and took her hand. "Now, do you want to be mad or do you want to go downtown?"

"I'm thinking." She folded her arms and stared at him.

"Let me know when you decide." He reached over and picked up a wooden spoon from the utensil holder. Dang, she meant to throw that away.

"I decided to go have fun," she said but gave him her best teacher look. "But we can't be late because I still have papers to grade."

"Good decision," he said, and put the spoon back in the holder. "We won't be late. Get your coat. It's chilly out."

"Yes, Daddy," she said as sweetly as she could. It was the

least she could do. Was she upset with him or what? She couldn't decide. Walking down the street holding his large warm hand, though, she knew, would be the best feeling she'd had all day.

"Good girl," he said. "Coat. Now."

Joni shook her head and giggled while she went to the closet to pick up the coat she'd just hung up. Okay, an hour at the square and then home to grade papers and she would sleep very well tonight. She didn't care if he knew where she was at all times. In fact, that could be kind of fun. There were some places in town that just might make him wonder.

"They are already playing," he said.

"Then we better run!" she said, and they both ran, holding hands and laughing, through the mist. This was the life she wanted, she thought. Nothing more. What would more even look like? What could be better? Living here in the sweet little town that did things like high school concerts on the square and her handsome hunk of a neighbor next door, a job she loved and dancing in the rain. This was the life she wanted. At least for the moment.

"Joni, what's going on with you and my brother?" Ellie looked across the table at her and Joni picked up her tea.

"What do you mean? There isn't anything new going on."

"You seem to be getting along better. There isn't so much on and off again as there has been." Ellie looked at her. "Things going better?"

"It was never not going better. I don't know what you are talking about." Joni stabbed at her pasta salad.

"Yeah, but something is just different, you know?"

Yeah, she did know but the reason why was nothing she wanted to talk with her boyfriend's little sister about. Things had settled down between her and Hank. His very unorthodox method of dealing with her, with them, their issues and relationship for some reason was working. She couldn't remember the last time she'd dramatically marched out of a restaurant or jumped out of the car or slammed his door stomping her way out of his house after he annoyed her.

"Maybe he's growing on me a little more," she finally said. "I'm not sure why but he's not as irritating as he used to be."

Ellie laughed. "That's weird. I have never thought he was irritating."

Joni rolled her eyes. "He's your perfect big brother, of course you think he's perfectly non-irritating."

"He's not," Ellie insisted. "He's the best big brother and he grew into a great man."

Joni rolled her eyes again. They were going to fall out of her head. "He's not that great."

"We can agree to disagree," Elle said. "Now, let's talk about the Christmas parade. It has to be the best one ever!"

"Why? I mean, I know you like things to be nice for the community, but why does it have to be the best ever?"

"Well, you know, Mike's wanting me to cut back on some of my projects," Ellie said wistfully. "And he's right. Sometimes I'm gone five nights a week and he's getting tired of it. He gave me a deadline to start cutting back."

"Or what?" Joni asked, suddenly fascinated. Did Mike... well, would he?

"Or what?" Ellie seemed puzzled by the question.

"You said you had a deadline to cut back. What happens if you don't?"

"Oh. I see. Well, when you are married you have to compromise on things. And, well, I do miss him too. So we decided it was best if I cut back. I don't think the Christmas parade will be one I cut back on. That's only a few months of work and you know he likes to ride the float and be Santa, so I hope I can continue, but, well–" She shrugged. "Anyway I decided to go all out on it this year, and keep copious notes so if someone else does take it over, they will know what to do and who to call."

Joni didn't think that was really the case. There was some kind of behind the scenes thing going on there and wondered suddenly if Mike 'persuaded' Ellie the way Hank did to her. Surely not. Her little firecracker friend who basically ran the town and all the events in it wouldn't put up with being put over a lap and spanked. Would she? Who knew what went on behind closed doors? It was certainly nothing she was going to talk about anyway, and so she switched the topic back to the parade as the young waitress refilled their tea. Once again, she found out, she'd be in charge of selecting which bands and floats and marching groups were where in the lineup and getting them all settled the morning of. She'd done it last year and it was fun, plus there was already a routine. The firetrucks came first, then a band, and of course, Santa and his sleigh were in the back, followed by a police car or two. So it wasn't that difficult, but just a little ego soothing for people who thought they should pick their spaces, and time consuming. That was okay, she had time.

She couldn't stop thinking though, as she walked back toward her house. As usual, her mind turned to Hank and his old-fashioned methods. He baked his bread from scratch and apparently disciplined his girlfriend as she'd heard they did back in the day. She'd read Outlander! She knew! Why did this spanking thing seem to work for her? Why? What was the deal with it? Grown women in this day and age didn't get spanked! Why did she stand for it? Their three month trial period would be up at the end of this month, just a couple more weeks and she'd agreed to go along with it till then. Then they would sit down and talk about it. Discuss if they were going to continue or not. She could stop it at any time.

She didn't even have to wait until the end of the month. She could do it right now, if she wanted. Why didn't she?

There was nothing she liked about the entire process. Not one thing. She hated the routine of carrying the quarter to the corner. She hated knowing what was going to happen when she lowered her pants and panties and let them drop to her ankles. Knowing what would be coming when she put the quarter against the wall and stood there, vulnerable and half naked and usually shivering with nerves. He thought she would be contemplating what it was she'd done, and sure, occasionally that flashed through her head, but usually she was just thinking about her upcoming spanking. How hard would he spank? How much would it hurt? Would she be crying before it was over? What would he use? Would he give her a warmup first or just start with the hard ones? Those were the hardest to take and usually meant that she'd acted quite a bit out of what he considered her normal calm happy self. She never knew, but knew she hated the wooden spoon and from somewhere he'd found a small leather strap that made her howl in a totally different way. Why did she put up with it? What was wrong with her? Think logically, she told herself.

Well, she liked the way he held and comforted her after. That was good and she always, oddly, strangely, felt safe and connected when in his arms. There were days after when his annoying little things weren't as annoying anymore. She never understood why, but figured she didn't have to. She also, weirdly, liked knowing that if he said it would happen, it would. He always followed through, no matter how much she didn't want him to keep his word. It would be fine to let her slack sometimes! Get away with something. Surely standing in the corner was a bad enough punishment! He didn't have to spank her too!

How would she feel if he'd stood her in the corner and then... nothing? That was all that happened. She'd feel relieved, first, then probably, if she was being honest with herself, she would be disappointed and rather irked at him. He always did what he was supposed to, or what was needed and required. Spanking her though wasn't one of those things, was it? No.

The more she thought about it, the more irritated she got with him. She needed a break from thinking so much, all the time, constantly about him and his methods. She didn't like his methods, so why put up with them? She didn't want a sore bottom. She didn't want to have that surge of panic when she didn't think she could take it anymore and when her fight or flight instinct kicked in. She hated how he kept spanking well past her threshold of being able to take it. She hated the loss of control and the mortification of exposing herself both in the corner and over his knee. In fact, she wasn't going to take it anymore.

Pulling into the grocery store, she got her list out and mindlessly went through the familiar aisles, her mind racing. Tossing items in the cart, she kept thinking and remembering how badly it hurt when he spanked and how she unabashedly tried to dance the sting out after while in front of him, rubbing her bottom frantically while her nose ran and her tears flowed. Why did she put up with that? She was a grown woman who had a good job, a nice house, a circle of friends, activities she enjoyed and was someone people relied on. She did not deserve to be treated like a tantrum throwing toddler. Why was she allowing herself to be treated that way? That thought wouldn't leave her head.

She self-checked her groceries, bagged them and put them back in the cart, realizing that once again she'd forgotten her reusable bags at home. See, that was annoying, but it wasn't anything she should be spanked over! Would he spank over that? No, probably not, she thought. She was trying to be fair, she reminded herself. She'd agreed to this. It wasn't his fault.

He just came up with the idea. She was the one who went along with it. She could stop going along with it now. Shivering as she went out in the late fall almost winter air, she loaded the groceries quickly in her car while it warmed up. It didn't take her long to get tired of the cold. Maybe she'd apply for an Arizona license and look for jobs down there. It rarely got cold in Arizona. How about Texas? No, she heard they recently had a deep freeze and Texas was so big. How could she pick where to go?

Why was she even thinking of moving? Oh yeah. Cold, not trying to dodge the next spanking. Right? Well, she'd done nothing to deserve one now. She didn't have to worry about it.

She drove toward home, hoping the heater would kick in quickly. It had gotten cold. What was she going to do? Thinking all the time was wearing her out. Making her stressed. Just like Henry did. Why was she with someone who stressed her out? She had a happy life. Her sister was safe. Her stalker was long gone. Her life, as she kept reminding herself was good. Was he the only stressor in it?

Her mind raced as she decided to not head straight home because the heater warmed the car into a cozy retreat she didn't want to leave, and instead to drive around the lake for a bit. Even though most of the leaves were gone now, the lake was still as gorgeous as always in a starker almost bleak kind of way.

Hank was a good man. He took very good care of her. He watched out for her and yes, protected her, even from herself. But he was the only one she acted out in front of. So if he wasn't around, she wouldn't need to be protected from herself. Absently, she parked and looked out over the lake, warming her hands over the heater vents. Still, calm, and although it was starting to turn winter gray today, it seemed to sparkle and exude serenity. She wanted to exude serenity! Why couldn't she? It all came back to Hank. What was she going to do?

Well, first, she was going to get the groceries home before the frozen stuff melted. Then, as she drove home, she smiled as she decided.

"You decided what?" Hank looked shocked as they sat together that evening.

"You heard me, genius," she said. "I'm tired of being stressed out with my mind racing all the time. Fix it."

"Fix your mind?" He looked sincerely puzzled. Maybe this genius thing was overrated.

"Yes. All I do is think. All the time. I keep going over options again and again. This... this thing we do," Joni threw her hands up in a futile movement, "is, I don't know, but it's all I think about. Is it right, wrong, why do I accept it, do I want it, why does he do it, are we going down some weird kinky thing where you will tie me to the bed and use whips and chains and I don't know!"

"Do you want to be tied to the bed?" he asked, obviously stalling for time, so she didn't even bother to answer but crossed her arms and glared at him.

"Fix it," she repeated.

"Joni, love, I'm not sure what you are asking me to do. If I could fix anything, and I mean anything, for you, I would. I just don't understand. I'm a mere male. Help me out."

"I'm tired of over thinking this, this, whatever this is."

"Okay. I understand that part. I think. Me holding you accountable for your actions makes you think about your actions?" He still looked confused and she was starting to get irritated with him.

"No! I mean, well, yes, I mean no. That's not what I'm thinking about. I'm thinking about you and us and this and why and I'm tired of it. My brain races all the time." Did that help him? Maybe this genius thing, well, how did she even know he was? Who said? Where was the proof? Certainly in this moment it was hiding.

"Why are you thinking about it? Is it like when you lose a tooth and your tongue goes there all the time till you get used to it? Do you think once you get more used to things it will be better?" He stood up and walked over to the fridge and opened the door, obviously, again, stalling for time. "Want a drink?"

"Juice please," she said. Was that it? Was she thinking about it because it was new? Like she thought about sex all the time when they first started enjoying that part of life? Now, while, yes, she thought about it, it wasn't always on her mind. Maybe that was all it was? Could it be that simple?

"It's been months, almost three," she reminded him. "We have a meeting at the end of the month to discuss this. I need a calmer mind before we do. I'm tired of overthinking this."

"By this, you mean me?" He still seemed to be trying to understand and she assumed she should feel grateful for that. Many men would have thrown up their hands already and walked away from an uncomfortable conversation.

"No. Maybe. I don't know. I am constantly just thinking about this, this…"

"Spanking thing?" He supplied for her and she noticed an almost smile when he put her glass of juice in front of her with a couple of his chocolate chip cookies. Both things irritated her.

"I didn't say I wanted cookies," she snapped.

"But you sort of do now that you see them, don't you?" he said picking one up and taking a bite. "They're pretty good."

He wanted to talk about cookies? She took a bite of cookie, which, of course was excellent, chewy and soft, just like she liked them. Of course.

"So all you think about is me standing you in the corner and then paddling your little butt and turning it red?"

Joni tried to blush and tried to hold eye contact. It wasn't easy. "Yes! And I want it to stop!"

"You want me to stop your mind from thinking?" he repeated and she was getting a little tired of it. How hard could this be?

"You are the genius. I can't figure out how to do it and overthinking it is making me stressed and unhappy. So, yes. Either I need to stop obsessing over this or we need to stop doing this." There. That was plain enough for him, wasn't it?

"I understand," he said, slowly, then took another bite of his cookie. The man was just flat out handsome, she thought. Suddenly, she felt a rush of warmth toward him. The last thing she wanted was to break up with him, wasn't it? Hopefully he didn't think that. Adoring, and yes, probably even loving him wasn't the issue. It was all the stress thinking about the spanking she may or may not be getting.

"Do you think that this thing we do, as you call it, is improving our relationship?" he asked, finally.

Was it? Did it? "I don't quite know how to answer that. I mean, sometimes. But why? Why should it? It's wrong. I don't like it. There is nothing about it I like."

"That's the point," he said. "To deter the behaviors you don't want to repeat."

"Well, if it worked, then it should have worked the first time, right? Yet, I've been repeatedly spanked and probably would be again, if…" She hesitated. "If we don't stop it."

"Is stopping it the goal of this conversation? We said we'd discuss that at the end of the month, if you recall."

"But I want to discuss it now."

"Because you are that unhappy?"

Joni stood up. This was going nowhere. "It's like you don't even listen to me!"

She got up and walked toward the back door, calling over her shoulder, "Think of a way to fix this!"

Intelligently, she did not slam the door on the way out as she left. See, apparently this thing they did taught her something. He didn't like slamming doors. She didn't like the consequences of slamming a door. So there was that. However, she admitted, she felt highly tempted to slam it. Instead she took a deep breath as she walked across the backyard to her own house.

Getting to her door, she realized she'd left her keys over at Hank's. Well, that was annoying. Very. The last thing she wanted to do was go over there again and get them back. But she didn't have a choice. Her house, as always, was tightly locked with the alarm system on. It would be nice to be able, at some point to live like she actually lived in this safe small town instead of a high crime area. But she couldn't. That was on Eli. She hoped he was far far away but also hoped he ran a red light or something soon and would get picked up and hauled back for some sort of justice. He'd gotten away with what he did to Beth on a technicality, but she hoped that Miranda's future lawyers would be extra careful. Sighing, she turned to go back to Hank's to get her keys and bumped into him. Standing behind her, dangling her keys in his hand, he said, "You forgot these. And this."

Swooping her into his arms, he kissed her like he had never kissed her before, tenderly, then more aggressively. Holding her tighter and claiming her mouth with his till she felt chills, shivering in his embrace. Desiring. Wanting. Her knees trembled and she felt her brain going fuzzy. What was this? Luckily he had a tight hold of her, or she felt she would fall, her head spinning.

"There." He pressed her keys into her hand. "Something else for you to think about."

With that he was gone, as silently as he'd arrived and she watched him go until he disappeared into the dark. Sighing, she touched her fingers to her what felt like swollen lips, then fumbled with the keys to get in the door. Half tempted to follow him back across the yard, she didn't. Instead, she went into her kitchen, and shut and locked the door behind her, and made sure the alarms were set. That was a habit now. What had he just done? Why had he done it? What did it mean? Why did she feel so discombobulated? What did he do to her?

Sinking down in the kitchen chair, she put her head in her hands. Obviously throwing this overthinking thing in his lap didn't change anything or help at all, did it?

Hank walked around the lot with his friend Max. "So thinking this is the one, huh?"

Max nodded. "Ben's coming out to look around and see where the best place to build will be. I'm glad you could come out too. You thinking of buying a place for you and Joni?"

Hank looked at him, startled. "Hadn't even occurred to me," he said. "Why, what did you hear?"

Max laughed. "I hadn't heard anything. If Lucy knows something, she hasn't mentioned it to me."

"Would she though?" Hank asked. Everyone loved his wife, Lucy, but really, she was an airhead. Although, she really wasn't, he'd learned over the years. She'd escaped from a very, almost cult like family and put herself through college. She got several degrees and while she did flit from job to job, she also worked as a day trader and apparently paid off her house and had a stash of savings. Max worked as an investment broker and yet, he'd told Hank once, he didn't have as much in savings as Lucy did with her administrative assistant jobs. She was a conundrum, but an adorable one with very colorful hair and a playful attitude that made everyone smile.

"Probably not," Max confessed. "She's very loyal to her friends, and tends to keep their secrets."

"I thought there were no secrets between husband and

wife," Hank said, walking around a very large willow tree. That thing would have roots everywhere.

"Everyone has secrets," Max said. "In fact, I'd probably be afraid to see and hear what all went on inside Lucy's cute little head."

"I'd agree with that," Hank said. "Joni is a baffling entity, also."

"Women. You guys on or off right now? Is that a hibiscus?"

"It's a rhododendron," Hank said. "Gorgeous spring flowers. I'm not sure."

"Not sure if you are together or not?" Max shot him a look that Hank understood.

"Yeah, I know. It's different. Do you always know where you stand with Lucy?"

"I do. We have a different relationship. Lucy is smart. She's intelligent but she has a short attention span often and needs some focus. I give her the focus she needs and a rock to lean against. My methods are unorthodox, but it works for my wife. You need to find out what works for yours. It may sound sexist but women, I've found, want their man to have some backbone and just not put up with some things. You know, save them from themselves so to speak. As long as they know they are forgiven afterwards."

Hank walked around, pointing out a few wild blackberry bushes that would be wanting to take over soon while he thought. Wasn't that what he'd been doing when he spanked her? He thought so. So what wasn't working? He was smart, he could figure this out.

"Joni is complicated. Then there is the Eli thing on top of that. I'm just not certain he's not going to come back for her. A man just doesn't up and disappear."

"Sometimes they do," Max said grimly. "I know if

someone hurt my Lucy, he'd sure as hell would never be found."

"I'd thought of that," Hank admitted. "I've wondered a few times if between Ben and Nick that's what happened to Eli. I wouldn't blame them a bit if so." He sighed. "And you know, that would almost be better than the worry he's going to come back here looking for Beth and find Joni instead. I actually found out she thought he'd been in her house and didn't tell me. I went crazy."

"That worry would make me kind of crazy, too," Max said. "I worry enough about Lucy's past catching up with her, but so far it seems to be leaving her alone."

"She is brave. It would have to be hard to leave everything you ever knew," Hank empathized.

"Basically that is what Joni did," Max reminded him. "She left a job she loved to move to a town she didn't really know, and no people she knew, with her little sister in tow to take care of. That took a lot of courage."

"I hadn't thought of that before," Hank admitted. Why hadn't he? He knew Joni and Beth had moved here to get away from Beth's situation. However, he had never thought of it from Joni's point of view. How hard that had to be for her. To leave her job she loved, family and friends behind, to move somewhere alone with her sister who had an insane stalker after her. She'd have had to be so frightened and overwhelmed so often. No wonder she acted out sometimes. She did need that rock to push against. Some stability, someone she knew would be her soft place to fall. He'd tried to tell her and explain to her that he was that person. Somehow he wasn't getting through to her though.

"This way," Max said. "I think there's some fruit trees back here. Not sure if you can tell what they are this time of year or not, but I'd like to know. Then Ben should be here any minute."

Hank followed him, still deep in thought, but looked over the small trees. "Not a hundred percent till they get leaves this spring but pretty sure these are peach and those are apple. You will have a nice little orchard here."

"Lucy wants cherries," Max said. "Guess I'll be digging holes."

Hank laughed trying to imagine Mr. Suit and Tie digging in the dirt. "Just call me. I'll come help. You could still plant them this fall if you can get some soon."

Max shook his head. "Nah, I want to do all the construction first, before I put in anything permanent. Appreciate your help. I have skills but knowing a weed from a plant I want to keep is not one of them."

Hank looked back toward the road as they heard a truck driving up. Ben probably. They walked back up the property. "Why are women so challenging, Max?" he asked, only half serious. As if anyone knew.

"That's what makes them so much fun and interesting. One thing for sure, my little Lucy never bores me. I never know what to expect with her. My reputation is that I'm a bit of a stodgy fuddy-duddy, you know."

Hank laughed. He knew better than to answer that.

"But Lucy, well, it sounds trite, but she simply lights up my world. Exasperates the hell out of me. She's too impulsive for her own good, but she's rock solid gold, all the way through. I might need to tamp down her impulses now and then, but I'd never break her spirit or try to make her be something she wasn't."

Hank didn't recall the usually taciturn Max ever talking so much.

"You and Lucy are a good match," Hank said, watching Ben get out of his truck. "A weird match. Never imagined you ending up with a woman with purple or green or pink hair who flits from job to job."

"Hey, she likes my dog." Max grinned. Max had a little yorkie who usually went everywhere with him. "She's home now, resting up from a teeth cleaning yesterday. Lucy stayed home to watch her."

"Well, what more could you want in a woman?" Hank laughed and said, "Hey, Ben, good to see you."

"Hi, Ben, hang on a minute, would you? I have to take this call real quick." Max held up his phone and then put it to his ear and walked away.

"Hey, Hank." Ben had his hands full of his tablet and some other things Hank assumed he was using to assess the building site.

"Ben. Keeping busy?"

Ben nodded. "Work as hard as I want to."

Would they address the elephant, Hank wondered? Why not? "Hear from Miranda?"

Ben half grinned. "Yeah, a few times. She's healing and you have her well placed. I don't know what I would have done without you stepping in. I wouldn't have had a clue."

Hank shrugged. "Sucks we had to figure things out the hard way due to the scum bag, but gotta keep the women safe."

Ben nodded. "And I owe you one. Anytime you ever need a favor or a helping hand, I'm here for you."

"I'll remember that," Hank said. "Though you know you don't owe me anything. If Joni were in trouble, you'd help if you could."

Ben nodded. "Keeping the women feeling safe, that's the important thing." Then he laughed. "Wouldn't our independent females be surprised we thought like that?"

Hank chuckled. "Yeah, they would probably be furious. I can take care of myself! But that's what we do, we can't help it."

He said his goodbye a few minutes later and started to

drive home. Keeping the women, his woman, feeling safe and protected. That was the key. That was Joni's entire issue. She needed to feel safe after so many years of being on edge. How did he not realize she had been? Did she even realize she was seeking a safe haven? How could he make that happen? That was the question, that was what he needed to figure out.

Joni shivered as she pulled on her coat. She was already ready for a quick faux summer which happened in the fall almost every year. A tease of summer for a few days before fall returned with a vengeance. Hopefully it would show up around Halloween so the kids could have decent weather for trick or treating. She'd already loaded up on candy and planned to spend the evening on her front porch, wearing the cat costume she'd bought about five years ago for a party in Chicago. That had been a really fun time, she recalled, smiling. Why did none of her friends have Halloween parties? Maybe she should? She had yet to host a party at her house.

The more she thought about it, the more excited she got. She'd invite all the teachers, her friends, basically have an open house. Trick or treat for adults! Why not? She could make some cute little gift bags, and buy some sweets from Jordyn, and bake some savory stuff. Just little finger foods. She'd send an email tonight. Oh, bob for apples? No, probably not. The thought of all the make up being washed off in the bucket didn't sound like much fun. Well, she could have a few other things to do to break the ice. Sighing, she wished Beth and Nick could come. Well, why couldn't they? Surely she would be safe here with all her friends around for one night? At least she could ask. No was a complete answer if she or Nick didn't feel it was wise. She'd ask though.

As she got in her car to head home, she got more excited. This could be really fun!

Picking up her phone, she called her sister then put the phone on the holder so she could talk and drive. "Beth! How are you?"

"I'm really good! How are you doing? I miss you!"

"That's why I was calling. I'm doing a little Halloween party at the house and want you to talk to Nick and see if you can come. You could spend the night in your old room, be home for a day or so. If you both think it's safe."

She could hear Beth hesitate. "I'll talk to him," she said. "I'm not sure."

"Only do it if you are comfortable," Joni said. "I won't be upset if you can't come, but I would love to have you."

"I would love to come back for a day or two," Beth said. "I'll see what he thinks."

"Good! I don't want you to come if he doesn't think it's safe, but if you can, that would be great! How is work?"

"Well, I've given my notice," she said.

"You've what?"

"Yeah, I found a graphic design firm that will let me work remotely and I'm getting back into that. I don't think anyone can trace me through my married name now, so it should be safe. Instead of Beth Sinclair, I'll be Liz Kinkirk. I'm starting over from scratch with my reputation, but I'm really excited about the opportunity."

"Bethie, that is wonderful! I know how much you missed doing that work! I'm so happy for you!"

After they hung up, Joni worried. Beth hadn't gone back into graphic design after Eli attacked her for fear he could track her work. He knew what she did. Surely, she was safe there now. He might not even be looking for her anymore. Then she flashed to the olives in her fridge. No. He was still looking for her. Leaving her presents. Was this safe? Should she call Nick? No. Beth was a grown woman. She made smart decisions and of course, Nick already knew about it. Anyway, maybe if they came to the party she could pull him aside and talk to him. She'd find out.

Right now, she felt the excitement build again, she wanted to get home, double check the date on the calendar and then send out the invitations and be committed! She pulled into her driveway and glanced over at Hank's. He wasn't home yet. Did he have ball practice tonight, she wondered? She wasn't certain, but it didn't matter. She had a party to plan!

Why hadn't she thought of this before, she wondered as she gathered her things to head into the house. Well, mostly, because they were flying under the radar for so long. It was all she could do to get Beth to allow handymen into the house, much less open it up to a gaggle of people.

Locking the door behind her and resetting the alarm, she looked around, checking as always, then rushed over to her laptop when everything seemed n place. No open or closed doors, no presents in the fridge. She was good tonight. After confirming the date on the calendar, she composed a little email, then took a deep breath and pushed Enter and Send. She was committed to a party! Shivering, there was a flash of *what if no one comes* but laughed at herself. Her friends would come. She'd have people at her party. Smiling, she looked down, yep, she already had two confirmations. Yay!

Suddenly, she wanted to tell Hank and get his input, and went to the kitchen window and looked out, he still wasn't home. Maybe he was over walking Mrs. Conlin's dog again. He often did that for her, and another neighbor when they couldn't get out or the weather was just too much for them. He was a good man, she reminded herself. Of course he was. Everyone knew that. Too good sometimes, yeah, but really, it was nothing he could help. If she was to continue in a relationship with him, it was part of him she needed to accept and embrace instead of fight against.

Yes.

Why hadn't she thought of that before. Like her sister Sydney would say 'concept'. Instead of fighting him and allowing him to irritate her, why didn't she just accept it? Realize the jerk was simply perfect and it was nothing he could help like Syd couldn't help her intelligence, and dry sarcastic sense of humor and Beth her talent for design. Their mom couldn't help being a workaholic and loving what she was so good at doing. It was just who he was. She knew that, of course, but it just hit her in a different light for whatever reason. He couldn't help it. She could help her reactions to it.

Shaking her head, she sank down in the chair and sent him off a text, *hey, stop by when you get home, would you?*

She didn't get a text back, but figured he was busy. He might even have a ball game, though she didn't think so. What should she do? She needed to kill some time while she was waiting on him.

Cookies. She needed cookies. Going to the kitchen, she got the butter out from the fridge, and put it on the counter to soften and then grabbed her grandma's recipe book to find one that sounded good. Peanut butter would be good, she decided and began the soothing, comforting ritual of baking comfort food. Sure, it was easy enough to go to Jordyn's and buy them but there was something about the smell of baking wafting through the kitchen that made people happy. Plus it occupied her mind and gave her hands something to do.

However, it wasn't working tonight. Her mind raced as she measured and mixed. Could she do it? Could she just accept him as he was, as he is, and not expect different from him? If yes, why hadn't she? If no, then why was she with him? That wasn't fair to either of them.

She pulled out the silverware drawer to look for the ice

cream scooper she used to scoop up the dough. What did he see in her? Apparently she frustrated him enough that he felt the need to spank her. Spank her! That wasn't normal, even if the internet thought so. What did the internet know, anyway? They were basically a bunch of people just like her, struggling to find their way but spouted it so everyone could see. Then those other people took it as gospel. It still didn't make it right or even proper.

So what was it with her accepting it, and even craving it now and then? She shook her head and finally scrounged out the scooper from under the pile of utensils. In his kitchen, he would have been able to open the drawer and put his hand on it without even looking. That was part of his perfection.

But no one was perfect, she reminded herself for the hundredth time. Maybe that was his fault? His perfection. Could that be a thing? Sighing, she put the first batch of cookies in the oven and then poured herself a big glass of milk in anticipation.

Hank pulled in front of his sister's house and parked. His little sister had done great in life, and he was very glad about that. She had started out wanting to be a realtor and excelled at it. Threw herself into Clearwater social life with everything she had and quickly became the go to person for all the events in town, from the Christmas parade to the Wiener dog race. Then she got tapped to work as a City Manager and she and her side kick, the irrepressible Lucy had uncovered a major financial scandal that was still dragging its way through the courts. She'd married very well, to a guy he really liked and they'd built this honking huge house. Ellie seemed happy and that was all that really mattered to him. Mike kept her reined in from overdoing, which she tended to do. Occasionally he wondered how his brother-in-law tamped down her enthusiasm for doing all things in all places, but decided whatever it was, it was working. That was all that mattered. He rang the bell and Mike answered. "Come on in, Ellie's almost ready."

"Thanks," he stepped into their well-appointed house and looked around, seeing Miranda everywhere he looked. She had done the design and the house was gorgeous. He hoped she was settling in and healing well in Zephyrhills.

"So, you are doing it, huh?" Mike said, leading him into the kitchen.

"Yeah, I figured why not?"

"Well, that's the best reason, I guess," he poured them both a glass of tea. "Ellie will be a few more minutes. We had a little discussion earlier and she's composing herself."

"All isn't right in Paradise?" Hank felt a twinge of alarm.

"Oh, it's fine," Mike assured him. "All settled and things are good between us. When you get married, you will find out every day isn't roses and sunshine, but you talk it out and get past it. We are in it for the long haul."

"Good. I don't want to lose a brother," Hank said, then turned as Ellie waltzed into the room looking adorable as always. He still saw her as his little kid sister who played jump rope on the sidewalk out front of their house with her friends, instead of the City Manager of Clearwater.

"Hey, Eleanor," he said, resisting the urge to ruffle her hair.

"Hey, Henry, I'm so excited! Thank you for asking me to go with you!" She slipped under Mike's arm and he absently kissed the top of her head, and he felt a little relieved at the naturalness of their affection. Whatever had happened was apparently over. A good thing.

"Thanks for helping me," he said. "I know a lot about a lot of things, but ring shopping isn't one of them."

"Lucky for you, jewelry shopping is something I excel at," Ellie said and smiled excitedly.

"Don't I know it," Mike moaned out with a smile. "Luckily you look adorable all sparkly."

Ellie giggled and gave him a hug. "I'll be back soon. You ready, Henry?"

"I am. Sure you don't want to come, Mike?"

"Nope, I'm good. Just bring my girl home safely to me soon."

"Will do," he said and they headed out to his car. Opening her door, he tucked Ellie into the front seat and then climbed in, and smiled at her, suddenly feeling nervous. "So you think this is the right thing to do?"

"I know it is," she said. "I have always wanted a sister and who could be better than Joni?"

"Well, you have Lucy," he reminded her. "She's almost your sister."

"Well, but now Joni will be legal!"

Yeah, she would be, wouldn't she? Hank thought as they drove downtown. He'd wanted her to be and to feel safe after her years of turmoil and this made logical sense to him. They basically were in each other's pockets all the time anyway. It wouldn't change things a lot. They would figure out where to live and what to do with the other house – or houses, if they decided to get one they picked out and chose together. He'd hate to leave his, but a new house might be a fun challenge.

Those were just details that would work out. Would she say yes? Of course she would. Wouldn't she?

"What are you thinking about so seriously?" Ellie asked him. "Do you think this is the right thing to do? Do you love her? I know your relationship has been, well, you've had some ups and downs."

"We have, but I think we're working through them," Hank said. "I am doing the right thing. It's just a step, you know."

"Well, it's the right step, my genius brother and since you are as smart as you are, then you know that, too."

"I do," he said.

"Good." She poked him in the side. "Keep practicing that. It will come in handy at the wedding. Oh! I get to help plan a wedding! I'm so excited about all this!"

"Maybe your next gig should be wedding planner," he said, pulling into a parking spot.

"Nah, I think I'm running for Mayor," she said, casually, as if it weren't a major deal.

"You are? Since when?"

She shrugged. "Lucy and I have talked about it for the last couple years since Mayor Lydia told me she was retiring. It would be step one."

"One of what?"

"One step on my way to President," she said.

"You aren't rich enough to be President." He tried not to laugh.

"Yeah, but I'm darn good at getting people to donate money and time," she reminded him. "I could manage. Besides, it would take a few years and Mike would have time to earn more money."

"How did you get all the ambition in the family?" he asked her, not even kidding. He knew he could have done much more with his life but what he had, suited him and made him happy. Now his sister, on the other hand, wanted to take every bite out of every single apple that life had to offer her.

"Just lucky, I guess," she said, climbing out of the car. "Come on, let's go pick out rings! Have you thought of how you are going to propose?"

Yeah. He had.

"So we are having a Halloween party?"

"Why not? I even called and asked Beth if she and Nick would come home for it." Joni looked so excited, he had to smile.

"Do I have to dress up?" She wouldn't want him to wear a couple's costume, would she? He'd have to put his foot down there.

"Of course you do," she all but beamed at him. "But you can surprise me if you want."

Good. No couple themed thing then. Whew. "Do you think it's a good idea if Beth comes back?"

She shrugged. "I honestly don't know. If we don't tell anyone and they only stay a few days, hopefully it will be fine."

"If they decide it isn't safe, then I'll take you out there for a visit soon," he promised. "I know you miss her."

She nodded. "I do. But I don't want to focus on that right now. I want to party plan!"

"How many people are you thinking?" He looked around the living room, envisioning it draped in crepe paper and spider webs. Sure. This could be fun.

"I figure maybe fifty but staggered, just thinking of it more like an open house where people can come, stay a while and go when they are ready."

"Fifty is a lot of people," he said.

"I already have yeses from over fifteen and I just sent out the invitation a few hours ago. Were you at a ball game earlier?" She looked at him, curiously and he debated about slipping in a little white lie, but decided that was ridiculous.

"No, I was out visiting Mike and Ellie," he said.

"Oh, that's good. I've not seen them for a while." Ouch. Okay apparently she was hurt because she wasn't asked.

"Spur of the moment thing." Okay, so that white lie slipped in. She'd be happy about it though when she found out why. But not yet. He had a plan.

"Oh, well, that's okay. I was party planning anyway. Two weeks! That's not a lot of time to plan."

"Not with our jobs, and having to find a costume," he agreed. "What day is it and where do you even find a costume?"

"Most stores or online," she said. "And the Saturday night before Halloween."

"That works. You just let me know and I'll do anything I can to help you." He smiled at her and then patted his lap. "Come here. I have a craving to kiss you."

"Yes, Sir. I can do that." She nestled into his arms and lap and sighed happily. "Love being here with you."

"Love you," he said, softly and held her tightly. Yes, the day before the party, he decided. That would be when he'd spring the ring on her and hopefully she'd say yes and could show off the sparkly thing that Ellie had helped him pick out. He turned her around so she faced him and started kissing her. Yeah. That was a good start to this evening.

He felt Joni's phone buzzing in her pocket and she pulled away to glance at it. "It's Beth," she said almost apologetically.

"Answer it. I'll pour us a drink." He headed toward the kitchen as she slid her screen open. He could hear her side of the conversation as he put on milk to heat for hot chocolate. It just seemed like a cocoa kind of night.

"Oh, that would be perfect, Bethie! I'm so happy!" Joni came into the kitchen as he was pouring the steaming chocolate into mugs and added a handful of mini marshmallows to hers. His didn't need any. It was perfect just the way it was.

"I take it Beth and Nick are coming to your party," he said, handing her a mug.

"Yes, she is!" Joni all but beamed and he felt a little bad that he hadn't realized how much she missed her sister. "She said Nick thought it would be okay, but he wants to bring a couple of his cousins with him."

"Bodyguards?" Hank guessed.

"I assume so, but hey, what good party couldn't use a couple extra men there?" she sipped her chocolate. "This is really good."

"You're welcome. Are you implying I'm not enough testosterone to make the party zing?"

Joni giggled with her adorable little melted marshmallow moustache above her lip. He reached over and wiped it off with his thumb and noticed her looking at him with her huge eyes. Suddenly chocolate was not what he wanted, and he took her cup from her, putting it on the table, reached over and slung her over his shoulder. "I'll show you testosterone, woman," he said, as he smacked her bottom and carried her upstairs while she giggled.

Chapter 6

Hank sat at his table and looked at the open ring box in front of him. Today was the day. He was going to do it. Did he have any doubts? Not really. He loved her. They'd been together long enough that he couldn't imagine life without her. So what was he thinking? Just that it was a big change. His life would never be the same again. That was a good thing, though. He always wanted a life here in Clearwater. A place where his kids would grow up, his grandkids would come and visit for the summers and recall their time with him and his wife, their grandma, with happy nostalgia. It was all he ever dreamed of, unlike his sister who thought she wanted to be president. Hank shook his head, smiling, at the thought. Well, if that was what she wanted, Mike would make a wonderful First Gentleman. The future was exciting for them both. Hopefully for Joni, too.

There was a busy day planned and he needed to get up and get showered and then get to enjoying his day. First his surprise proposal to Joni, then home and wait for Nick and Beth to show up. After that, they'd go out for a late lunch with a small surprise celebration he had planned for her. She had fretted last night that she really needed to decorate and work on her party but he'd told her a quick early breakfast was just what she needed before working all day. She'd agreed begrudgingly. Maybe his surprise would delight her. He hoped so.

He looked through his clothes. He shouldn't get too dressed up but a tie with his buttoned down shirt seemed a nice touch. Trimming his beard, then brushing his teeth twice, he slipped the ring box in his pocket and headed over to wake his soon to be fiancée.

Unlocking her door with his key, he frowned to see there was no coffee made, nothing that looked or sounded as if she were up and getting ready. "Joni?" he called. No answer.

That was odd. She knew they had a date. His heart hammered a little and he took the steps to her bedroom two at a time, trying not to think of anything or everything that could have happened to her. Knocking loudly on her closed bedroom door, he walked in, calling her name.

Relief washed over him as he saw her in bed, stretching and moving around. "Overslept, did you?" he asked.

"What? What time is it?" She sat up and looked around.

"Almost seven," he said. "Come on, we have plans."

"I guess I stayed up too late working on party things," she said. "Hank, I really don't think I can go out with you this morning. I just have so much to do, with the party and Beth coming with her entourage." She blinked at him and ran a hand through her sleep tousled hair. He half smiled. She would be his wife and he would see that adorable sight every morning. She scowled at him. "Why are you wearing a tie? Where were you taking me?"

"Where am I taking you," he corrected "I just felt like it added a festive touch to the morning."

She frowned. "I'm not dressing up. I have things to do and don't want to be changing fourteen times today."

Hank sighed. Nothing was ever easy with her. She couldn't even go to her own surprise proposal graciously. "You can wear what you want. But I figured with Beth coming and things, getting a little fancy would be a nice gesture."

She rolled her eyes and sighed, then whined, "Hank, I have things to do."

"Joni, get up. Get ready and I'll meet you downstairs in fifteen minutes, unless you want to spend the day rubbing your sore rear."

She snorted, rudely, he thought, at him but rolled over and put her feet on the floor on the side of the bed, while he went downstairs to make a pot of coffee so they could have one to go. He had no qualms reddening her cute little butt before they left, but he'd rather not. He grinned and thought of another idea. Well, he'd just see her mood when she came down. He had the coffee poured in travel mugs before she made it down. Found her purse and put it on the table and checked his watch. They should have plenty of time.

She stalked down the stairs a few minutes later and he silently handed her the coffee. "Let's go, Sunshine."

"Henry, I swear," she started.

"You swear and me and your cute butt will have a discussion," he warned, grabbing her purse. What did women keep in these things that were so important? With his other hand, he grabbed his coffee and headed to the back door. "Let's go."

He held the door open and she walked out, wearing a nice pair of jeans, sneakers and a new sweater he hadn't seen before. It was a green color that made her hair stand out and her eyes look gorgeous. He liked it. That would work for today just fine. He locked the door behind them, after making sure the alarm was set. That was their new normal and while he was glad they had it, he hated they had to do it.

After they were settled in the car, she sipped at her coffee and almost sighed. Maybe she only needed some caffeine to put her in a better mood. He hoped so.

"So where are we going?" she asked. "I'm not sure I'm even hungry yet and I can't be gone too long."

"You will be fine," he said and noticed her scowl as she sipped her coffee again.

"You better help me get ready later then. I could have a lot done if I didn't have to be here."

"I know. I'm so cruel, aren't I? Forcing you to eat and have a little break before 48 or more hours of other people being in your house and cleaning and cooking."

"Now you understand," she said, and sipped her coffee again.

Driving toward their destination, he saw her scowl coming back. What was with her? Oh. She didn't know what he was planning. Of course. Well, all he had to do was get her there. No matter what it took. She'd be happy then. He hoped. If she didn't jump out of the car. She'd done that before too many times and he wasn't going to tolerate it again. With any luck, she'd drink her coffee and settle down. Today should be a good day. He needed it to be.

"I'm going to help you with the party things, and making beds and decorating and whatever else you need," he informed her. "I just wanted to give you a little treat before things got busy."

Weirdly, that didn't seem to set her mind at ease, because she scowled at him again. "Did I ask you for that?"

"Am I not allowed to do things spontaneously at all? Aww, come on, just tell me you are enjoying the view." He waved his arms in front of them.

"Where are we going? I thought it would be Debbie's Diner or Baking Memories, not somewhere out of town when you know I'm busy today." She gulped the last of her coffee and put it in the holder. "And I'm going to need to pee soon."

Great. He hadn't anticipated that, but, he smiled, thinking. Actually that would work out well.

"I'll stop in a few minutes," he said. "If you can wait that long."

She nodded and stared out the window.

He drove another few minutes till they were in a wooded area, that would have been lush and green a few weeks ago, but now was sparse, the leaves almost gone. Soon it would be winter. He didn't mind winter. Long winter nights, researching his book next to the flickering fireplace. Lots of homemade stews, soups and hearty casseroles. Skiing when he could get a day or two away. He loved all the seasons, which was another reason he loved living where he did. They all had their perks. "Here," he said and pulled over to a quiet spot off the deserted road.

"Here, what?" she said. "Oh, you want me to rent a tree?"

"You can do it. You've done it before," he said encouragingly.

"Fine." Joni undid her seatbelt and glared at him. He was right. She'd gone behind a tree often and it was no big deal to her as she knew it would be to some other people. Half smiling, she thought of her mother and the horror on her face if she had to use the woods as a bathroom. Getting out of the car, she threw back, "We'd better be close to this place and it better be worth it. You don't realize how stressed this trip of yours is making me."

Not looking back, she made her way into the woods and found a fairly sticker free spot to borrow a tree and quickly accomplished her needed task, then walked back toward the car. What was he thinking today? Sure, she was as spontaneous as anyone else, but really? He knew she was having four people spend the night at her house tonight and things needed to be done for that. Then there was the party she really wanted to overdecorate for. Sure, Beth would help her tomorrow, but still, there was a lot to do. And he wanted to drag her off, traipsing through the woods, and then to some hole in the wall diner? Why? What was going on with him?

Marching back to the car, she felt herself working up to a righteous, well, what he called, a fit. It had been quite a while since she'd jumped out of the car and slammed the door behind her, stalking away. But she was really tempted right now, to do just that. Her anxiety was ramping up, and then there was the niggling worry about Beth's safety coming to town. Who wouldn't be anxious? It was normal and… "What are you doing?" However, as hard as her heart started pounding, she knew what he was doing.

"Going to help you relieve your anxiety," he said, way too calmly for someone slipping their belt out of the loops on their pants.

"No."

"Don't recall asking," he said and snapped the belt, making her shiver. "Drop the jeans."

Joni shook her head. "No. I won't."

"One. Two."

Her fingers scrambled for her jeans button. "Wait, wait!" She never wanted to know what would happen when he got to three. It wouldn't be pretty, she knew that much. Not that this would be. "What did I do?"

"You just need a reminder to calm down and this is the fastest way." He snapped his belt and she shivered.

"Aww, come on, you don't have to. I'll be good," she said as she slowly lowered her zipper knowing there was no way to get out of this. "I'm not stressed!"

"So lying on top of being pouty and whiney? Little girl,

you are aching for a good whooping if I ever met someone who was."

She shook her head as he motioned to her pants. No. She did not want to do this. "What if someone sees?" She stalled. They were well off the main road and this road didn't look as if it got much traffic.

"Should have thought of that earlier," he said. "Let's get this over with so we can have a good day."

"I want a good day without a sore butt!" She lowered her pants anyway but left her panties on. Just in case someone did drive by. Hopefully he'd let her. She looked at him uncertainly, not sure what to do. She wasn't taking her shoes off in the woods and it would be hard to walk with her jeans at mid-thigh. What did he want? Well, that was his issue, wasn't it? She looked at him, and forced the most pitiful look onto her face she could, realizing that suddenly she wasn't stressed at all about overnight company or the party tomorrow. Only about that belt snapping in his hands.

He strode over to her and grabbed her upper arm, and swung the belt. She felt a sear before she realized what he was doing. Though, she knew what he was doing, it still didn't really make sense in her brain. Her jeans around her knees hindered her movements but she tried to do an awkward dance shuffle away from him. "Hank! Stop! No more! Please, please!"

The belt kept rising and another stripe of heat lined her almost bare bottom and upper thigh. "No! Stop!" Pulling away got her nowhere and she felt her pants fall further down her legs which didn't help the desire, the need, to move out of reach. "Ow!"

She was going to start cussing in a minute, she just knew it. It hurt and was so mortifying she didn't think she could deal. "Hank! Henry! No more. Please!" The belt continued to fall while she danced as well as she could trying to get away from

116

it. "I'm sorry! I'm sorry!" She couldn't help the tears that fell while she twisted and squirmed and shuffled her way around and around. His hand had a firm hold on her arm and she couldn't get away. All she could do was dance as awkwardly as she ever had, trying to get away.

Finally it occurred to her to just collapse, as well as she could with his hand holding her upper arm. Falling to her knees, she realized the belt had stopped and he'd let go of her. It was over. She bent down and sobbed. Realizing what she must look like with her panty clad bottom sticking out behind her. But who cared? Not her. Vaguely over her sobs, she heard his belt click back into place where it belonged. Thank goodness. However he didn't say anything, just let her kneel there and cry. Why?

No one can cry forever and eventually her bout of it wound down. He leaned down and helped her to her feet, then pulled her close and gently rubbed what felt like welts on her sore, hot bottom. Clinging to him she whimpered in pain, but oddly felt a huge sense of relief.

"Feel better?" he asked.

She shook her head violently against him, trying not to soak his shirt or that tie he wore for some weird reason, but said, "I guess."

"That was a resounding maybe," he said and smacked her butt. She scrambled to pull up her pants over her hot swollen bottom.

She did feel better but sure wasn't telling him that. That was the thing about spankings. They absolutely did not feel better during, but cleared the air and lightened her spirit after. Why? She didn't know why. It just was the way it worked and she wasn't going to complain. Except during. Then she was going to complain a lot. However, that was his problem to deal with, now wasn't it?

"Good. Let's get you in the car and get your face cleaned

up." He took her hand, instead of her upper arm and led her back to the car.

"I don't want to sit down," she whimpered. "You hurt me."

"I know I did, and part of your punishment is to sit on your sore little bottom." He tucked her into the car and then got in beside her. "However, you only have to sit for less than ten minutes."

"We're almost there? Why didn't you wait and let me go to the bathroom there?" she asked, trying not to squirm.

"Because I didn't want to," he said.

"Well, that, of course." She laid on the sarcasm as thickly as her almost hoarse voice could manage while wiping her face. "Of course that is the best reason."

"It is, oh, here we are," he turned off the road and onto another side road and she felt totally confused. What was out here?

Then she looked up ahead. There was a hot air balloon.

Joni held her finger out to her sister Beth. "And then we went up in the hot air balloon and he proposed! There was champagne and strawberries and…"

"And you said yes!" Beth squealed. "I'm so happy for you. For you both! What a gorgeous ring! Did you pick that out yourself, Hank?" She looked at him suspiciously and Joni laughed.

"Bet Ellie helped, but who cares? I love it and I'm so happy!" The two sisters jumped up and down, hugging, while the four men watched them, smiling.

"You have to give me all the details, later," Beth said. "But I need to freshen up some. Oh, these are Nick's cousins, Lucas and Connery."

Joni looked over at the cousins. Wow, they grew them big in Zephyrhills, didn't they? Both were at least six two and almost identical. "Twins?" she asked before she thought but when they nodded, she walked over and shook both their hands. "So glad to meet you! Thank you for coming. Did you bring a costume?"

"Yes, ma'am," one of them rumbled. "We did. Glad you can have us here."

"Having handsome males at a party is always a perk," she said, turning to hug her brother-in-law. "I missed you, Nick. Thanks for bringing Beth home, safely."

"Congratulations, Joni," he said, pulling her into a hug. "I'm so happy for you both. Now I get to plan a bachelor party."

"Well, not yet," she said, taking Hank's hand. "We haven't worked out any details yet. I'm just excited about the party tomorrow."

"So am I!" Beth said. "It's been forever since I was at a party. Well, since my wedding anyway."

"That counts!" Joni reassured her. "Come on in, guys, I'll show you your room and then we're going to have lunch at the Rushing Water. It's a seafood place. Then you guys can go do what you want while Beth and I party plan."

The twins exchanged a look and Nick said, quietly, "We aren't leaving Beth alone. At least one of us will be with her at all times."

"They said I could use the bathroom alone, though," Beth laughed and Joni could tell she was trying to make light of a serious situation.

"Oh." Joni felt embarrassed. She hadn't thought of that. Of course, they wouldn't. That was why they were here. Just in case. "That's okay. We can do most of it from the house. I'm sure my fiancé will be happy to run out shopping."

"He would," Hank said and laughed, grabbing her hand

and kissing it, then looking at the guys. "Her fiancé also has a couple cases of beer and a pile of burgers to grill at the house later tonight."

"Sounds good!" One of them spoke up. Connery or Lucas? Hard to tell. Joni figured she'd be able to tell before they left in two days.

"One of us can stay here," the other twin spoke up. "Take turns."

Joni and Beth shook their head simultaneously, and Joni said, "I have a state of the art alarm system and you will be right next door. You can check on us all the time, but you might as well have fun while we decorate." She turned to Beth. "Mike is bringing Ellie over to help us, too."

"Great! A pre-party party!" Beth said, and flipped her now much redder hair back off her face. "Want to call Jordyn?"

"Her mom is sick and she's going over there as soon as she gets off work," Joni told her. "But her sister is taking over tomorrow, so she will be at the party."

"Hope her mom is okay," Beth said. "Okay, I'm off to freshen up. I assume the guys are in Syd's room?"

"They are," Joni said, watching all her company disappear upstairs. She turned and rushed to Hank, who had his arms out and seemed ready for her attack. She jumped into his arms. "I'm sorry I was so crabby this morning."

"It's over." He kissed her forehead. "Punished, forgiven, non-issue."

"That's one of the things I love about you." She kissed him. "You don't hold grudges or make me feel bad afterwards for being a jerk."

"I know my girl," he said and put her down. "I'm just glad you are less stressed. Oh and said yes."

"You were worried?" She giggled at the thought.

"Hey, not sure I'd marry someone who belted my ass." He put her down as they heard feet on the stairs.

"Luckily for you, you don't have to," she said, turning to greet her guests. It would be a great couple of days.

Joni pulled on her black cat costume that she'd tried on a few days before, just to make sure it fit, before she had it cleaned. It did fit and made her feel sexy and strong and she loved it. Hopefully Hank would like it. What wasn't to like? She turned and finished up her makeup, then scampered downstairs, because of course, a kitty didn't walk. They scampered and pounced and slunk and well, occasionally they walked regally, of course, but tonight she was in scamper mode. Her house had been transformed into a spooky hideaway. Dark mood lights, spiderwebs, a skeleton Ellie had dug up from somewhere stood in the corner. There was the requisite Monster Mash and other spooky songs on repeat on some kind of sound system Hank had hooked up. What would he be wearing?

Connery and Lucas were twin Bigfoots and they had door duty. Nick had mentioned that if Eli wanted to sneak in tonight, a costume party would make it easy. Everyone was in a mask or made up. Who would notice? The hope was that seeing the monsters at the door might deter him, however. She couldn't figure out how he would hear about it, though, and felt certain he was states away making someone else's life miserable.

Beth and Nick came down in a prince and princess outfit and she had to stop and stare at them. Beth had come such a long way since she had gotten married. Zephyrhills was so good for her, as was Nick. She was almost the old Beth she'd been before Eli. Almost. The old Beth and she hated to think it, had been a little arrogant and sometimes a little hurtful but not on purpose. Now, however, her true empathetic soul shined through and she was as beautiful inside as out. Nick, of course, was a real prince.

Just like her Hank who showed up as the sexiest pirate she'd ever seen. Wow. "I wish I was a parrot now, instead of this," she told him, taking him in.

"You want to sit on my shoulder, do you?" he asked,

"Well, somewhere," she said. "You look great."

"And while you look absolutely adorable, I can't wait to get you out of it."

"You are funny," she said and turned to grab the cold finger food from the fridge. "Can you get the cauldron for me so I can make the punch, please?"

"Whatever you need, my kitty cat," he said. "Who is bringing the dry ice?"

"That would be your sister and she is picking it up on the way, so it will be fresh."

"Fresh dry ice sounds weird," he said.

"Dry ice is weird," she said. She'd researched it and found she could put dry ice in her cauldron, it would sink to the bottom and while it would steam, it was safe for the drink itself. You just couldn't eat the dry ice itself. "But weird is the theme for tonight, right? Well, and showing off my ring."

"I'm glad you like it," he said.

"Love it." She held out her hand. "Worth every bit of that belting."

"You are funny. There goes the door, people are coming."

Jordyn and Ben arrived in the kitchen carrying boxes. "Here's your sweets!" she called. Jordyn, dressed in a white chef's outfit, set the box down on the kitchen table. "Where's the platters and I'll plate them up."

Joni looked over at Ben dressed, of course, as Paul Bunyon. "Did you two even try at all?" She laughed, and put the platters on the table.

"We didn't have time to go costume shopping, so we used what we had," Jordyn said. "It's my busy season and I have a wedding to plan."

"So do I," Joni flashed her ring.

Jordyn looked over at Hank and said, "About time!" And then hugged Joni. "I'm so happy for you! We will have to coordinate our weddings so I can make you the best cake! Now, where is Beth? I've not seen her in forever."

"In the living room with her Prince Charming, I assume," Joni said and got started placing the themed pastries on the platter. Jordyn had, of course, done a great job.

She looked up and saw Ellie and Mike walk in and cracked up. Mike, dressed as Abe Lincoln, escorted the cutest Uncle Sam she'd ever seen. "You two are amazing!" She laughed. "I love it!"

"Welcome to the family," Mike said. Ellie had been here last night and had already seen her ring, but Mike took her hand and gave it a solemn once over. "Very nice." Then he turned to Hank. "Where's the beer?"

"Let's go bring it in," Hank said. "It's getting chilly out there."

"What can I do to help?" Ellie said. "And you look amazing, by the way."

Joni did a little pirouette. "Thank you but I think it's the rock."

"I want to see the rock!" Lucy danced into the room, looking so Lucy like, as always in her Glinda the good witch costume, but Glinda's hair was never that color! Pink, blue, purple and that had to be glitter all over it. She'd be picking up glitter for months! But, it was Lucy. What more could anyone expect?

"Here's the rock. Where's Max?" Jordyn held out her hand.

"He's out with the guys drinking beer and pouting because I made him dress up as Haggrid." Lucy giggled and some of her glitter floated around the room. Joni laughed. "Did he even know who Haggrid is?"

"Not a clue, which makes it even more fun," Lucy said, then turned as Beth came in the room with Jordyn.

Jordyn couldn't believe what proper, prim and strait-laced Max would do for her crazy friend Lucy.

"Beth!" Lucy danced over and hugged her. "How is married life and the new town? I saw your new cousins. I swear, if I wasn't married…"

"They are adorable, aren't they? And I love where I'm living and my new job. I was just telling Jordyn I used her portfolio as part of my resume to get it."

Joni looked around the room. When she moved here a few years ago, would she have thought this would be her life? A job she loved, friends she adored who would do anything for her, and a man who wanted to marry her. If Beth were completely safe, life would be perfect. Beth was as safe as she could be in Zephyrhills though and had a lot of family to take care and watch out for her. The last few years had been filled with drama and laughter, tears and joy. Who knew what the next few years would bring? More adventure for sure. While she had a feeling that some things would stay the same, like the friendship of the women in this room, there would be many changes ahead. She slipped under Hank's arm as he showed up next to her and smiled her kitty kat smile at him, wiggling her whiskers.

"Hey, baby, we have more ice?"

Yeah. They had more ice, a party and a life here in Clear-water to enjoy. Together. She turned around and kissed her handsome genius. This man, this life. It was all hers to grab with both hands.

The Kinkirk Clan series - Coming Soon.

What is the mystery in Zephyrhills and why do the Kinkirks congregate there? What brings women to their town for protection?

Megan McCoy

Megan McCoy lives in the heartland of America, surrounded by corn, soybean fields and hot guys on tractors. At home, she's raising kids, Chinese Cresteds and poodles, training them all with a tender hand and heart, while saving her sternness for the alpha males in her books. Getting up at three in the morning to write leaves her time for a few hobbies - gardening, canning, bike riding, bread baking and taking in strays.

Don't miss these exciting books by Megan McCoy and Blushing Books!

Clearwater Romance series
The Wife He Wanted
The Wife He Adored
The Wife He Needed
The Wife He Protected
The Wife He Corrected

Hometown Love series
Don't Mess with Jess
Hannah and Hawk
Totally Tori
Kelly's Haven
Hometown Love Collection

Her Choice series
His Firecracker

The Dilemma
The City Girl
Her Choice, Always
Her Choice Forever

South Dakota Dreams series
Stormy's Trouble
Talia's Time
Wynter's Waif
Wynter's Wife
Sailor's Search
South Dakota Dreams Collection

Along Came Jones Series
Sebastian
Hank
Logan and Ronnie
Logan's Contract
Along Came Jones Collection

Single Titles
Two Weeks of Joy
An Old-Fashioned Relationship
Hard Wired Desires
Quinn's Comeuppance

Anthologies
12 Naughty Days of Christmas 2016
12 Naughty Days of Christmas 2017
12 Naughty Days of Christmas 2020

Audio-Books
An Old-Fashioned Relationship

Connect with Megan McCoy
www.meganmccoy.com

Blushing Books

Blushing Books is the oldest eBook publisher on the web. We've been running websites that publish steamy romance and erotica since 1999, and we have been selling eBooks since 2003. We have free and promotional offerings that change weekly, so please do visit us at http://www.blushingbooks.com/free.

Blushing Books Newsletter

Please join the Blushing Books newsletter
to receive updates & special promotional offers.
You can also join by using your mobile phone:
Just text **BLUSHING** to 22828.

Every month, one new sign up via text messaging will receive
a $25.00 Amazon gift card, so sign up today!